Edi

Alice Jardine, Harvard University
Susan Kirkpatrick, University of California, San Diego
Olga Ragusa, Columbia University, emerita

White

Spirit

Paule Constant

TRANSLATED BY BETSY WING

University of Nebraska Press : Lincoln & London

Cet ouvrage publié dans le cadre du programme
d'aide à la publication bénéficie du soutien du Min-
istère des Affaires Etrangères et du Service Culturel
de l'Ambassade de France représenté aux Etats-Unis.

This work, published as part of the program of aid
for publication, received support from the French
Ministry of Foreign Affairs and the Cultural Service
of the French Embassy in the United States.

Library of Congress Cataloging-in-Publication Data
Constant, Paule.
[White spirit. English]
White spirit / Paule Constant; translated by Betsy Wing.
p. cm. – (European women writers series)
ISBN-13: 978-0-8032-1535-1 (cloth : alkaline paper)
ISBN-10: 0-8032-1535-5 (cloth : alkaline paper)
ISBN-13: 978-0-8032-6441-0 (paperback. : alkaline paper)
ISBN-10: 0-8032-6441-0 (paperback : alkaline paper)
I. Wing, Betsy.   II. Title.   III. Series
PQ2663.O575W5513 2006   843'.914–dc22   2005016481

For A.E.G.

And out of the ground the Lord God formed every beast of the field and every fowl of the air; he brought them to the man to see what he would call them and whatsoever man called every living creature that was the name thereof.

Genesis 2

Translator's Note

White Spirit, in addition to the usual impossibilities of translation, presents a particular obstacle: many key words (starting with the title) are already in English – American English. Once they rejoin the colonizers' language they no longer mark the problems of colonization. Sometimes a translator will put words such as these into a language different from the "target language," even translating them back into the language of origin in order to make them "foreign" to the new reader. It is important, however, that the English words in *White Spirit* remain English because they represent the postcolonial colonization of Africa (and other parts of the world) by Western (especially American) ideas and culture.

Examples of Constant's use of this technique are too numerous to list here; in general, however, the English words retain a slight sense that they are odd and out of place in the context of Africa – and even in a French context. For instance, the brothel is named the "Sunset," and the French woman who runs it has taken Lana Turner and Marilyn (no last name needed!) as her models of beauty. (To be blond and light-skinned is highly desirable in Africa, as the lengths the heroine of the novel will go to achieve this prove.) The fine madame earlier had a career at 20th Century Fox, which she calls "Fox," and she swears by a beauty manual written by a Miss Priddy (how French hears our "pretty"), who long counseled women who turn to *Reader's Digest* for advice.

Victor's stock at African Resource provides the prime example of things that don't belong. It is made up of vast quantities of items that no one else in the world wants, and it is his task to make them desired in Port-Banane. Cans of sardines from Brittany (overstock, perhaps), electric toasters where electricity itself is not standard, exploding pressure cookers, carcinogenic or flammable baby clothes, and the mysterious powder that becomes White Spirit itself. And there are others . . .

Another word is important to mention in terms of the postcolonial culture of Port-Banane. It is a holdover from former days when colonies were achievements to be proud of since it was, after all, the will of God that brought white men to "civilize" Africa. It has echoes for us in our own postslavery culture in the South. The word is *boy*, and it easily moved from British colonies around the world to those ruled by the French. It means, quite simply, a male of any age who is obliged by his position of subordination to do whatever you say.

A final burst of Hollywood optimism seals this novel, which has teetered between tragedy and comedy on its way to a happy ending – the last chapter, entitled "Happy End." Whereas in English we easily retain a sense of the activity implicit in a verb when we transform it into a noun, French idiom would prefer a straightforward noun, such as *conclusion*. The movie title "The End" took primacy over Constant's likely acquaintance with the fairytale notion of a happy ending. The great burst of applause, the promised life of love fulfilled so dear to Hollywood films of this period are here in "Happy End." At the movies you would have seen it there, looming large on the screen:

THE END

White Spirit

The Will of God

The name of the boat was *The Will of God*. It jogged back and forth trafficking in one thing or another, black or white, between Africa and mainland France. Sometimes it was a "love boat" for the works council, sometimes a hospital boat for "charity business" – no matter what, it was a heap of junk. The undersides of the vessel took on water but, because it was in the captain's interest, it went right on trafficking. It was also advantageous to plenty of others: planters, dealers, or civil servants who lived attached to its carcass like shellfish eating rust, scrap iron and catastrophes. That's a big boat, said Victor's grandmother, and what's more it has a beautiful name.

Victor had answered a classified ad. An import-export society was recruiting energetic young men willing to take on responsibilities for its African branches . . . Since no diploma was required and the trip over would be paid he didn't hesitate. Sent off a self-addressed, stamped envelope and now was keeping an eye out for the mailman. He could see him coming a long way off as he started his route on the corner where the Favre house stood. He propped his bicycle up beneath its windows, between the striped petunias and the climbing geraniums, then stopped off for a little chat in front of every house. Victor was losing his patience. But his grandmother (he hadn't heard her coming) was right there behind him, letter in hand already. She had been to the post office to get it; she had opened it: he was hired; he was leaving on the fifteenth of the month.

He would have to have an outfit. They took the bus to town. Grandmother wore her Sunday best, pocketbook in hand and real garnet earrings, head high, the picture of pride. The whole way

1

there she listed the things she'd buy and untangled the thread of fate for him. Her imagination was adventurous, her notion of things epic and sacrificial tempered by a great desire for bourgeois respectability. She acknowledged the world's order and accepted heaven's; consequently she was able to discover the signs of a divine plan everywhere and in everything. He liked how she told him his life the way people read lives in cards. How do you know all that? he would ask. It's because I'm old, she replied, and he understood that twenty isn't old enough to foretell one's future.

They went into all the best stores, well-established shop-keeping dynasties with mosaics on their pediments, wooden counters, and drawers with copper handles – establishments that specialized in underwear or uniforms or hats or suits. She walked ahead of him and, mesmerized by her broad black back, he followed behind just as he had followed ever since childhood, like a little duck. She told his story again and again until he could have recited the saga of his future success by heart. As a result it became the truth. Still it was taking a great deal of work to convince the saleswomen and persuade department managers, whose assessment was that the old woman's preamble was as long as her funds were short. It seems to me, she said, that these establishments are nothing like they used to be. Not welcoming. Remember: in a business the client is king. So they made do with department stores. At Conchon-Quinette's they succumbed to the voluble pressures of a salesman dressed like a mannequin who had immediately grasped the scope of the undertaking. Grandmother chose a black suit for him, thick and heavy and just perfect for confronting the wear and tear of a life of daring at the same time that it provided the austerity and seriousness lacking in someone so very young.

He put it on to pay his respects to the Favres, the ruling family (with a hotel, a grocery, a snack bar, a restaurant for traveling businessmen, a gas station, plus everything else – a cabinet maker's shop, a whole slew of farms they sharecropped). They had the village to do their work and Grandmother at their beck and call. You have to take your leave of them, she said. So they went there, but this time he was in front and she followed behind. She thought he looked handsome. Move along so I can see you. She wasn't seeing – she was drinking, devouring. She couldn't get enough and her earrings quivered and wriggled like shiny fish. She stopped in front of the cross that the Favres had erected in the very center of the square, in the shadow of their house, as a sign of their conquest, and seized by an attack of fervent confidence, the sort that ends up in a song of thanksgiving and a grateful prayer, she crossed herself. Alleluia, she said.

They didn't go in through the shop the way they usually did but instead went through the guest entrance reserved for great occasions, with its mirrored coatrack and the copper bucket she polished every morning. A woman's voice called out, Who is it? but didn't come out to look. Grandmother shouted back: It's the boy, he's come to take his leave; she herself didn't count. The voice yelled that since it was Victor he could just as well have come in through the grocery, especially since she was alone there and couldn't just leave the customers. Absolutely obliged to go in through the store.

Grandmother, thought Victor in his black suit, deserved the living room, a chair, Monsieur Favre himself, and perhaps a glass of Lillet, not the grocery store and one of the Favre girls, one wearing an apron no less and asking from a distance: What are you here for? He's leaving for Africa, the grandmother replied. Ah! said the young lady, and from the way she said Ah! you might have thought this was a catastrophe she'd long seen coming. She could see the servant's grandson locked up on Sing-Sing, or Cayenne, or Devil's Island a lot easier than she could imagine him on Salvation

Island. She was so convinced of the worst that she didn't even ask what he was going there to do. She gave him a sidelong glance. All that black bothered her; it didn't bode well. Another of the Favre girls came in. Same question, same response: Africa made their minds go blank, and they were stunned by his suit. The grandmother, before reeling off her supply of answers, waited for them to ask some questions at least. None came, but then, yes, what they wanted to know after all that was whether the grandmother might not have a little more *free time* after her grandson's departure, if she could give them a few more hours' work at the shop or the snack bar, *relieve* them. She said yes. The young ladies breathed easy again.

She never complained in front of him; she simply shrank down around her humiliations. Completely lethargic, overcome by a soft and happy passivity, Victor noticed that the garnets dangling from her ears were like dark drops that turned her face yellow and made her look sad. A trusting and languorous torpor muddled the dismay he felt and kept him from feeling much. The Favres' reception did not seem any more hostile than before, no different from the time he had made his first communion when they had also had to go in through the shop; he had even had to stand in line with the housewives and, what's more, the young lady on duty had attacked him because if it hadn't been for his communion the grandmother would have been working that day instead of her: I'm at the end of my rope! Too much work! until she caught a glimpse of the white silk armband he was wearing, which triggered a smile, and her hand hesitated over the cash drawer, then resolutely moved in the direction of the candy jar. What he kept from that day was the parsimonious gift – right there on his tongue, first the communion wafer and then the orange candy. Grandmother had said thank you.

He had earned his diploma, but that had been no better at

4

opening the door to the Favres' living room. Just didn't happen – no more predictable than the heat on that particular day. However, they had almost seen the square table where Monsieur Favre wrapped packages, the piano and the two leather armchairs protected by antimacassars made of English embroidery; they were really close. They had gone all the way down the hall and then, to avoid an open walkway that might have taken them to the kitchen, the grandmother had bumped him with her hip into a blind corner. Too late. Behind them a voice called through an open window that they should come into the garden and admire the summer crops planted by the gardening daughter. From behind the beanpoles came congratulations less enthusiastic than those earned by the tomatoes, a specially obese and crimson variety, that they were made to admire. He was way behind the carrots, the strawberries, and the fond expectations they held for an apricot tree that had branched out the year before. His manhood was particularly lacking in great occasions; it was merely a period of waiting out an unmitigated mediocrity that was witness to a parade of every conceivable failure. His grandmother had high hopes for his military service because of the uniform. But then – no service – his category was exempted. It's still lucky to have some bad luck, said his grandmother.

She was stubborn and, despite never having traveled so far, she wanted to take her boy to Bordeaux on the pretext that it's always better to be introduced by one's parents. She was the mother, the father, the grandfather; she was his entire past and he was her future. She would vouch for Victor – brave, hardworking, and honest. Honest above all, with the honor of the poor. The grandmother would have had herself cut in little shreds for honesty. To make her point she would have demanded certain tests: the ring left behind on the bureau, the coin forgotten in a pocket, the lost billfold she would find and return, the change she would hand over down to the last penny. Bordeaux was the last thing she would be able do for him, last because of her age, last because of her condition. Even though she wore the garnets of better days in her ears, the city revealed what she was: a peasant woman – but not one of the self-possessed, steady, and domineering sorts; she came from the underrace – humble, enslaved, and fearful. She felt dizzy.

They sat down to wait for their appointment in a bistro across from the docks at a Formica table where the flies were having a field day. They asked for coffee because that was cheaper, even though (she leaned over and whispered in his ear) it was far too expensive for what it was. She suspected it was made with dregs, something apparently done in the large cafés. The Favres' customers didn't know how lucky they were. She was torn between fierce pride and quivering humility, between wanting to criticize everything and wanting to be submissive. It embarrassed her to be served and she kept saying thank you. She would have liked to wash her cup and return it to them clean. Victor, without thinking and surprised at how easily he had caught it, squashed a fly.

Monsieur Beretti, director of this and president of that, all of which was printed in fake engraving on a business card pinned to his door, met with them in his bedroom. The grandmother had no idea that you could do business in the presence of an unmade bed with a man whose striped pajamas stuck out from under a paisley-printed polyester robe. There was a standing mirror, tilted a bit, in which their slightly elongated figures were reflected. Hotel rooms made her lower her eyes; she didn't like to serve breakfast in bed, for example. This big shot always did business like this; he'd left the offices, the secretaries, the whole kit and caboodle back in Africa. Here he was just a transient; the less time he stayed the happier he'd be; he knew better. He would be going back with his directors.

Director – the very word was dazzling. She had heard right: Victor would be the director of one of the branches of African Resource. She wondered if this wasn't maybe too much; she had come along with an apprentice and they were making him boss. But she didn't have to worry: African Resource trained its people. Then came a long discussion of how diplomas were perfectly useless, especially for anything practical. It's very simple: he, Beretti, an ex-student of the most prestigious engineering college, wanted nothing to do with them. As for conditions . . . She exclaimed that, after the confidence he had just placed in them, the conditions should be whatever suited him. Beretti turned to look inquiringly at Victor. Whatever she wanted was fine . . . So, shall we celebrate? Beretti ordered something to drink. It was hot already, but they turned him down out of habit, the same habit that made them always say no to anything pleasurable so as not to be obligated.

She felt sick; her legs refused to hold her up and a veil of sweat moistened her face. Africa seemed less terrifying than Bordeaux. The big city wore her out. Beretti magnanimously offered her the armchair so she could rest a bit. That way they would have time to watch how he handled his business. Phone calls made standing, walking back and forth. Two tons of insecticide? OK. One ton vitriol? OK. One ton rat poison? OK. One ton caustic soda? OK. One ton lemon-rub? Quèzaco? He looked at them to see if they knew what that was. I don't know, said Victor. Beretti shrugged his shoulders. Well, you, Madame, certainly ought to know what it is. Something for washing, for cleaning, for bleaching. Clorox? replied the grandmother, who was feeling a bit more like herself. No, there's the word white in it. Whiting, white lead, whitewash . . . a whole parade of words, all of them white or having to do with white, soaked white, bled white. No, no, said Beretti. Salt, the grandmother went on frantically, Epsom salts, smelling salts,

7

spirit of salt . . . No, no, frowned Beretti . . . White spirit? said the grandmother in a sudden burst of inspiration. That's it! he said, pointing at her as if to fix the word right there in her mouth, that's it: *white spirit*, anything American works great over there. OK for the lemon-rub, he said to the person on the phone. After that he refused every other suggestion because, like the boat, he was plumb full, couldn't take another thing. You're going to have tons of stuff to sell, he said to Victor with a big wink.

She wanted to accompany him all the way to the end. She walked beside him; she wanted to carry his suitcase so he wouldn't get tired, and also she still had a lot to say to him. But she couldn't remember any of it. All that came out of her mouth was a hymn of confidence in Victor's skills, about everything he'd do, everything he'd see, everything he was about to start. It was as calm and sweet as when she listed the charms of his forehead, his beautiful eyes and mouth. The feeling of being completely loved like the day when she had taken his shoes off and held his feet in her knotty, veiny, too-big hands, already old-looking, he'd thought, to warm them up. He had realized that his feet were objects of perfection, marvelous things. Then, overwhelmed, he had kissed her ugly hands to erase the distance of beauty and love that was too great between them.

She undid the garnets from her ears, put them into his hand, and squeezed it. Her head was ringing like a bell, in turns empty then full with everything she had said to him and repeated, full of useless things and abandoned by anything essential in a great muddle of emotion, with a great deal of despair and infinite amounts of confidence, with happiness and sorrow, enthusiasm and fatigue. Then, there, on the edge of the docks she had raised her eyes and said: That's a big boat, it has a beautiful name.

The Voyage

From the gangway all he could see of the sea was a thin gray trickle, oily and iridescent, opening and closing between the dock and the hull of the boat. No time to turn around – instantly into the depths of the boat and knowing nothing, just trotting behind Beretti. An iron door with holes pierced through it to let in the air. Sixteen berths, eight each side of the washbasin, no porthole: Gentlemen, your cabin! And Beretti went back topside.

Then there was pitched battle: one group wanted the top bunk, others appropriated the lower one, in the name of absolute and opposite principles, and the others took what was left. Bags every which way. Men who at first were enemies would suddenly ally to hang on to their places. Now installed, that is to say hunched half-way over their gear, they gave some thought to the situation. They said: The world's gone crazy! This is the white slave trade! They lit their cigarettes, just to blow a little smoke over what was happening to them.

They hated France, Europe, and the West, and though they didn't say they liked Africa, everything would lead you to believe they did. In this minuscule cabin, on this narrow bunk, deep inside the boat the same way other men are in the earth, corpses, they were recalling their meager lives. They had all been endlessly constrained, rushed, restricted. For them everything had been too small, too stingy: bistro tables, the contents of glasses and the contents of minds. To say nothing of neckties, the symbol of their social and physical suffocation. Neckties were accused of having bound them hand and foot and having strapped them down, while at the same time, quite the opposite, they were losing their money the way you lose blood. I've been gypped. Money just ran through their fingers. They bragged about how they'd sold every-thing. They had no regrets, sure to get back on their feet, *pronto*, ready to get rich: losers, rigid and compromised.

The boat creaked. A noise, strange jolts. Stiff winds, a storm, a black squall, said some of the others who had been to sea before. Enormous movements. Victor couldn't always tell whether they were going from front to back or from left to right; some temporary adventurer identified the directions by name from the depths of his bunk and was immediately challenged by another privateer who had Victor completely mixed up with his ports and starboards and swells and other pitchings-around. Some of the days were dreadful.

For him to know where he was someone would have to tell him, but then an instant contradiction coming from the third lower berth would put him several nautical miles to the north. Victor sat there dumbfounded as if somebody had stopped the engines to wait for directions from the bunk across from him, which then suddenly sent him off course, not just a few miles to the south but also closer to the shores, near enough to touch. He was afraid of shipwreck but then wished it would happen, to have some sky, some sea, some sand. He knew almost all there was to know about shipwrecks when you are the sole survivor, waking up on a beach with waves lapping at your face, the cries of parrots flying up like arrows into the sky. But *The Will of God* was avoiding the honeyed coasts, heading offshore into shadows and darkness, out where there is no bottom to the ocean. Which would mean being lost, exhausted, your hand clenched tight to an empty barrel, not slumbering lightly, deep in the sounds of a seashell, but endless death by drowning.

All things considered, it was better to follow the itinerary of the guy across from him, who was scribbling on his wall. First he drew some lines, curves that he erased with the back of his hand without

Victor's thinking any more about it than whatever you'd usually think about graffiti – that it was something dirty and forbidden. One day something about how the man looked from behind made Victor notice that he had stopped his endless scribbling. There was a perfect circle in front of him. Victor thought it was obvious, it was what it was, and gave it no more thought, the way you don't give the sky or sun a thought when you get them back. Not a day went by that the silent and taciturn painter didn't add something to his sketch or embellish it. He expanded his circle, adding thick hinges, huge trompe l'oeil screws – a superb mechanical drawing, perfect and useless as a masterpiece by a fine artisan, a porthole looking out on nothing. Then, gray over gray, he sketched in the sea and the sky; he drew in the horizon, and the sea separated from the sky. His traveling companions realized that something was going on. They took peeks, they made comments. They asked him if he was going to put in seagulls. He shrugged his shoulders because it was too soon. Seagulls, in fact, wouldn't arrive until later, at the same time as a thin gray line – nothing particularly recognizable. Then, in the distance, there had been a small boat. It wasn't until much later – they had just gone through a storm – that they caught sight of the first palm trees. That made them really happy and they could no longer contain their impatience; they gave all sorts of advice. Now that the other had done all this work, they had something to say about everything they had not imagined; they were critical. But Victor was delighted because it was Africa, just the way he had always imagined it. The artist rolled over on his back and closed his eyes. His silhouette traveled alongside the porthole.

Sometimes Beretti would stick his hairless head in through the half-open door; as they traveled on it grew darker and darker in color – reddish tan, dark as a brick. He used to come around to check on the cargo; he feared there might be broken barrels in the hold, somebody dead somewhere. But no, everything was fine. They craned their heads in his direction; hollow-eyed, blue-bearded, they forced themselves to smile. They hoped something about his gaze would give them a clue. Beretti told them it wouldn't be much longer, but nobody knew whether he was anticipating the end of their lives or the end of the voyage. Then he shut the door with a bang. It stunk inside there, an acid odor of suffering like the smell exhaled by battery chickens, something gone bad, something extremely painful.

You had to wonder how air circulated through the boat. The air that reached them must have come from the shuffleboard deck, where people were using the ends of sticks to push wooden disks around on a hopscotch pattern marked with numbers. It had come through the Chambord Grand Salon, the Surcouf Bar, the Beaugency Dining Room: white table linens, brandies and liqueurs, cigars and aromas. It had been through all the luxury cabins: Russian leathers, evanescent powders, floral essences just behind the ear, exquisite droplets in the hollow of a wrist. Then through the tourist cabins, where sea was replacing sky in the porthole: rubs of eau de cologne for cleanliness, stale lavender. The air had stagnated in the kitchens: insidious vapors, lingering mustiness, fetid belching. Little air, no more air, or just that leaking from the machines, full of noise, like paint refusing to set and soft so you can pick it off with the tip of your fingernail. Air half oil and half sweat, taken in with your eyes closed so as not to weaken it and without moving so as not to waste it. Eyes on holes someone made with a drill. Voyaging in apnea.

The travelers in the depths were obsessed (more and more so as time went by) with resurfacing, following the thread of air back up to the croquet deck, getting into the lifeboats and, underneath their canvas covers, becoming watery, windy, and starry stowaways. At night they took turns watching the spectacle of the wealthy. Through real windows, on screens as luminous as

movies, they saw a diplomat in boxer shorts, a disheveled indus-
trialist, a governor with no shirt on, just to have a sense of their
being just like everybody. A man, a woman, silent warfare, looks
like daggers. Or nothing, a woman dreaming in front of her mirror, a man staring off into space: the woman putting some color
on her face, the man putting on his tie; behind them stewards
were straightening things, cleaning and picking things up; they
folded the bedcovers, drew the curtains.

And then? asked the guys down below. They exchanged cabin
numbers; some were more interesting than others – young
women, even blonds. Up there young women were few and far
between and they had been able to observe that the blonds were
usually fakes. Victor thought he would enjoy looking at the night
and the stars, catching a glimpse of the phosphorescent swell
from under the canvas cover. But there was too much shadow, too
much water, too much darkness everywhere, and, turning his
back on all that vastness – the colossal dark, the bottomless water,
the enormous sky – he warmed himself by the spectacle in the
glowing square. He would rather have a window frame, a porthole's circle, a keyhole, something he could bear – not the whole
vastness of the world bearing down on his back.

Through the window where he lay in wait he saw a couple. He
could make out that their bodies were naked, which held his attention. They were on opposite sides of the cabin. The man was
staring at the woman, who was partly stretched out on her bunk
with her legs spread. Then he swung his head and torso heavily in
that obstinate way bulls have when they are about to charge. He
took three pounding steps, shaking the mirrors, and went for
her. He got back up immediately and did it again. Then he lay
there, crushed, motionless, exhausted. The woman slowly
crawled free of him and then, before Victor could realize what
was happening, she stood there next to him, outside on the deck.

She was naked, slender, with very dark, very long hair hiding her face and breasts. So close that he could have touched her. Mute with fear, curiosity and astonishment, he said nothing. He heard her breathing heavily, she was out of breath. He began to breathe irregularly out of sympathy. He was panting. Blinded by the darkness, she had not yet seen him, but she could feel his presence because of his breath and his odor. Not moving a muscle, not afraid, not ashamed, in an oddly weary voice, with the burnt-out gesture of a streetwalker, she asked him for a cigarette.

Victor had never seen a naked woman – moreover he didn't smoke. He was certainly sorry. He dug around in his empty pocket in vain to show he meant well, so the girl's request wouldn't be too humiliating. But she was blasé; already having turned her back on him, she leaned her elbows on the rail, closed her eyes, and offered her face to the damp rumblings of the sea. He saw her hair flying in the wind, her thin back, her round buttocks, and he couldn't get his breath back. She turned her back on the rail, shook her head, her hair; he saw her breasts and he choked up, he went all weak just above his knees and his hands were cold. She went toward the door to her cabin. She looked at him; he lowered his eyes. The door closed; he felt relieved.

He tried to see her again through the window. She was standing in the middle of the cabin; he noticed the bulge of her belly, the tip of her breasts, and in the hollow between her thighs an abundant, curly fleece. The guy had raised his head and was looking at her too. He lifted himself on his elbow and awkwardly swung his fat body upright. Seated with his hands between his thighs, he studied the girl. She stayed standing and, almost animal in her suppleness, she scratched her right calf with the tip of her left foot. Now that he'd seen her Victor couldn't look at her anymore. He'd had a look, now he was in love.

Angel or fairy. He discovered that the only words he had to assess her beauty were ones that hid her breasts beneath a bust, that rounded shapes off and mutilated the chest, removing that ravishing excrescence, all taut and pointed, that he had caught sight of just now. They were words that shaved off the body hair, leaving bodies like large, smooth, pink ghosts; words extinguishing smells with violet perfume; words that disciplined hair with hairdos and with a turn of phrase made buttocks into a unit, a mass disguising the line at the top and the dark separation. He had seen where it grew round, the curve turning inward toward depths of which he was beginning to have some inkling. This woman was neither an angel nor a fairy. He had no word for saying what she was.

In the cabin he tried to shut up about his discovery, but his secret burst out. He found it was no longer his. The guy in the sixth, despite being ready to go ashore, got his pencils out again: a vamp beneath the palms. All the men stood glued to his berth; the slightest line unleashed passions as if, by tracing it, the pencil really touched the organ it was drawing. Following the ins and outs of a sensual geography whose every least shiver, every least sensation they remembered, they cried out with pleasure. Not there, not there, they moaned, because *there* for them, *there*, was like a caress; it was too much. The vamp looked at them the way vamps look, her arms crossed behind her head, lifting her hair. The men were critical: tits not big enough, not enough ass, not enough slit. They were getting aroused. They liked pictures that were comical, preferred them to photos and, of course, to real women . . . Forgetting the girl, they gave a harsh account of the other side of the experience represented by women. They ended up with brothels. Victor was watching. Victor was listening. It was all rolling around inside his body – not seasickness, but still, he felt sick to his stomach.

What's that? Beretti asked, pointing to the girl on the wall. It was the last time he visited, the time he swore to them that this was the end, really the end. They explained and gave him the map and the cabin number. Being such good friends, they urged him to go see for himself. They couldn't believe it either. But that guy and the girl did it all night long, jumped each other, on again, off again, and never got anywhere, all with the same bullheadedness on the part of the man and the same resignation on the part of the girl. They were imitating love. Beretti didn't know the girl. But he knew who the guy was and believe you me, he didn't find it amusing. All of a sudden the men in the cabin shut up. César, César Di Marino himself, the boss of the Devil's Banana, two thousand acres of banana plants, the mayor of Port-Banane in person, the pimp at Sunset, the master of *The Will of God*. Watch out, guys, that's nothing you want to know about, he told them. The fellow in the sixth berth hurriedly drew some clothes on the vamp – a bikini.

César

César Di Marino's sexual potency was in decline. Specialists were very pessimistic and predicted it would be a more or less long-term disability. It had been several years now since they had suggested he undergo an operation whose complexity the surgeon had perhaps greatly oversimplified in his explanation. Something about a plastic penis. The way César saw it, plastic didn't have a good reputation; he felt it implied domesticity. He might have accepted a gold penis, or a silver one, or ivory . . . but not plastic. It seemed to him that you shouldn't expect much of an orgasm from that particular material.

Seeing that his patient seemed dubious, the surgeon was more specific: he was talking, in fact, about a small balloon. A balloon? César's imagination abandoned the hardware store and turned in the direction of toys. Naturally he saw light toy balloons, soccer balls in net bags, big hot-air ones escaping into the sky, but also loud punctures, the shame of going soft, disastrous leakage, pathetic moments of weakness . . . No, absolutely not, no balloon; rubber brought with it too many potential fiascos. He knew this from childhood experience; his father had popped his big purple one with the tip of his cigarette. Thanks a lot, it's the sort of temptation you'd rather not carry around with you. He remembered it as an almost fleshly violence that had set him (knee-high to a grasshopper) against that father, who then later had popped like the balloon from a perforated intestine.

He consulted a psychiatrist, who listened to him absentmindedly. It seemed his was just an ordinary case. You're not doing any fucking? So? So, so, César muddled on. You poor old thing, you aren't fucking like 50 percent, what am I saying? Like 75 percent, and even, according to the latest statistics, 85 percent of the population. Think about it, said the shrink, you're not fucking: like children and old men, just how many of those do you think there are? You're not fucking like exhausted businessmen, like the anxious men who took early retirement, like unemployed men who have run through their benefits. How many more is that? You aren't fucking like husbands who are already tired of it, like harassed young fathers, like immigrants living without their wives, like postal workers after a few years of service . . . You aren't fucking like everyone else who's not fucking and you want to fuck like the infinitesimal minority who do! Accept the inevitable, old man! Some medicine, doctor, begged César. Medicine! Nothing doing, said the shrink, who was sick and tired of pulling out his prescription pad. All you have to do is quit drinking, quit smoking and, he added, having forgotten the reason for César's visit: quit fucking.

Despairing now as any sick person who sees the limits of medicine, César put all the blame for his illness on science and quacks

17

and turned to alternative medicine for help. He got hypnotized. They didn't have much to offer except the promise of a red glow that he never saw and a warmth in his lower back that he didn't feel . . . The osteopath, full of self-confidence, proceeded by affirmation: You are seeing, you are feeling, you . . . No go. César didn't say no, they wouldn't have believed him, so he said yes, paid up, and didn't go back. They stuck needles in him more or less everywhere, until he looked like a golden porcupine. Nothing. He took a great many rhinoceros horns, tiger claws, tortoise shells, shark teeth, elephant tusks, swordfish swords . . . he began to feel like his body was becoming a Noah's ark.

In desperation he decided to take annual treatments at Vichy. Whisky and the women you meet at spas, desperate and in a hurry: it was all or nothing for them, and, in the same way others bet suicidally at gaming tables, they would have liked to drink until the springs were dry. They met men who had had fine careers, former diplomats and old administrators come to treat their beer bellies. They would extract some compliment, some gallant gesture from these men, whose brains responded with a reflex action that left them confused and distraught, completely amazed at having been able to meet the demand, gauging just how many decades it had been since the last time. The men arranged rendezvous by the fountain but the future brides, treacherous beneath their despair, would always dump a wheelchair for a cane or a nice, quiet house in the suburbs for an apartment on boulevard Saint-Germain and run off with the one who was richest or most spry.

This being the context, you can see the success a César Di Marino could have; his external handicap boiled down to a stiff arm and a mutilated hand (equipped now with just its thumb and little finger) caused by a hunting accident. Conjugating life in the present tense, he jogged on over to Cèlestin Springs with a terrycloth towel around his neck, in love with nature and vast spaces. He ran a classified ad in which he offered a trip to Africa and promised "real life" and marriage if compatible. In exchange he required sexy beauty, sweetness, and age twenty-five maximum. He was incredibly successful. Women by the dozens swarmed to this sticky trap at the Café de la Gare where he arranged to have his rendezvous. They came from everywhere, not finding the "sexy" or the "twenty-five max" much of a hindrance. Lawyers, physicians, teachers forsook their offices or schools for his sake: aching hearts, lonely mothers. He was their last hope. They liked everything about him, his title (chairman and CEO), his age (fiftyish: hale and hearty), the Voyage, Africa, Marriage, and "Real Life."

Right away, on their first date, he led them off to bed and diligently faked Doing It with them, taking however much time it took. Not one acted surprised. Some of the women had orgasms. They were incredibly indulgent; they found a thousand excuses for him and whispered a thousand promises. They were more reassuring, though just as ineffective, as the doctors. They assured him that it was better that way, without anything, far the most practical. He had carted off a few of these amazingly willing women. On the plantation they were called the Ladies and people were a little afraid of them because of the almost sexual frenzy they applied to social relations. They used the entire time not spent reveling in sexual pleasure to nurse the sick, teach the children, and loudly insult anyone and everyone. Basically, what they found most intolerable – even more than César's impotency – was Africa . . . They didn't hold up for long. "Real life" crushed them; César took them back to the boat. Some of them demanded to be sent back home on a plane. The prettiest ended up at the Sunset, Port-Banane's nice brothel – something to do with being cut out for the job.

His treatment was almost over and he had not yet found the woman he would take back with him this year. The woman of the moment, whom he was to recognize by the newspaper she carried, seemed somehow both so uptight and so wild that he decided against going over to her. He sat in the booth across from her and watched her for two hours. She powdered her face twice and put on lipstick three times, looked at her watch twenty-two times, and fidgeted her legs incessantly. Finally she left with the air of an insulted goddess. He had drunk four whiskies.

A very young girl replaced the annoyed one on the leatherette seat. Not choosy, she finished off the glass and swiped the change. She was a young bargain hooker, still soft, slightly dirty, slightly drab, but there was something touching about her. He was amused at her efforts to get some coffee money. They're reduced to that just to get five francs! he thought. He left a big tip in the saucer, which the waiter quickly pocketed. So, you're leaving, Mister César? He was leaving and he wasn't sorry to be ditching all this. You're lucky, the waiter went on, you're going to get back to the sun . . . At the word *sun* the girl became electric. César pretended not to look at her; he kept on talking to the waiter: space, real life, Africa. The waiter knew just how miserable he was, how crushed by the weight of the coffees he had to serve, by the winter, by the rain. The girl in the booth was going nuts. Not all of it's like that, said César as he stood up, but I have to go get my luggage . . . He glanced over quickly, just to see if she'd taken the bait. She jumped right up.

She followed him with the astonishing ease of abandoned dogs, taking the sidelong approach of an empty belly, keeping a feverish eye on him, fearfully at first, a few yards away – and then since he hadn't chased her away, right beside him. She's hooked tight, he thought, gratified. She spoke to him, something low and husky. He didn't answer; he was letting the sticky trap harden. They went through the beautiful park that runs along the Allier River. Light filtered down through the trees. Sun! This was a little girl's game, one, two, three, sun! She followed him, he turned around, she stopped. He was going to get to the river; afterward it would be too late. César was having fun, how would she say it? How would she offer herself?

But tell me, you, and he took her by the shoulders and in the twilight tracing shadows on her face he looked at her; she closed her eyes. He peered, the sun broke through the branches. You aren't? and the girl's mouth opened as if to show her teeth. He pulled her hair back . . . you are, huh? You are . . . it's France. That's what makes you gray, and the girl's eyelids fluttered and light trembled on the tips of her lashes. Heads or tails? Tails she was black; heads, white. Some people thought she was black but pretty. Embarrassment, tears, a misdeal, Africa and the sun staked and lost in one throw. She remained silent, suddenly no longer the strength to follow the rich man; poverty leaked out there in the formal park, behind a tree.

She was a black woman with no Africa and no sun, a black woman from Vichy, Allier, a black woman . . . white. He thought about his buddies and burst out laughing when he imagined their faces when they saw her. Laughing made him have to piss, which provoked a titillation in his prick that reminded him vaguely of desire. He felt a free-running, syrupy urge fade away at the tip of his penis and his mouth moved into an O around his astonished exclamation. You win, he said to her. Come on, don't wear yourself out, you're going, you're coming. It'll make the guys laugh. It was time. Mister César's luggage was already waiting in the front hall of the Relais Sévigné. The girl, her arms dangling down beside her faded jeans, a wicker bag at the end of a leather strap that she carried on her shoulder, was ready. There was a flower sticking out of an arrangement; he picked it and gave it to her. And what's your name? Lola, she replied, and already her voice was different.

Port-Banane

The sun, at least where The Will of God landed, was brown and more brown; the water was mud, the earth melted, a vast swamp lapped beneath an ochre sky. Towering above all that was a slag heap, a gigantic alluvial heap, a brown, gelatinous, putrid mass flowing to the sea in a long viscous river, a bank of rotten bananas. The smell – unspeakable.

Then they saw César on the luxury deck waving his arms at this mountain of shit. He was shouting: filth, filth. At first glance this word seemed the right one, adequate and not exaggerated, but despite its universality, feeble filth was unable to encompass that as well. Terrifying, outrageous, a horror when you got right down to it: three months of banana yields, a continuous, profuse, inexhaustible, obstinate yield which, at the other end of the world, had run up against a no less determined, stubborn, stupid, relentless, rabid strike of dockworkers. Filth wasn't for the bananas, it was for the dockworkers; there the word took on a moral ring. But for the mountain of rotten bananas what words were left? The barrier of dockworkers, the mountain of bananas, and between the two the ocean. Putrefied bananas flowed into sea.

Basically, on the other side of the ocean, the banana had never really caught on. However much they were turned into flour or liqueurs, or mixed with cocoa or wheat, or dried, it was impossible to camouflage the taste. You could just see consumers hesitating before the fruit basket, the brave one undecided about how he would attack it. Then there were all the cook's manipulations: cutting it up, crushing it, mixing it in to make it disappear. But the taste remained, unsinkable, even in fruit salad. No matter how it's disguised you find it immediately: one banana, just one, and the salad is off. Banana is all that's left in your mouth, everything else goes down but there's banana stuck to your tongue. One final hope – banana flambé, purified by blue flickerings of alcohol. But fire, even when consisting of rum, doesn't neutralize bananas; when the flame goes out the problem is still unresolved, sweeter than ever and more viscous.

Faced with the vast banana plantations, the world was like a diner who at the end of the meal can't bring himself to start on dessert. There were too many of them. Too rich, too copious, sickeningly sweet. The banana stayed on the shores of Africa while the West amused itself with other goodies. The dockworkers pushed the banana back into the sea. But the world went on blindly producing them. Banana Men disgorged them by the thousands of tons; they chose the best land, the most productive. They had eliminated the biennial pig-banana in favor of the anytime-anywhere banana that grew everywhere no matter what season, bananas galore – a banana anarchy, a banana menace, throwing the ecology, the economy, and society into disarray. More and more bananas. No season no earth no sky, just bananas, *bananas, bananas,* nothing else. The Banana Men didn't give a damn; caught in a vicious spiral, they didn't want to know that over there nobody wanted any more bananas. They'd had enough.

In Mégalo, people were so suspicious of the banana – which had already ruined the roads, sent finances into a tailspin, and destroyed the climate – that they wouldn't let them in through the freight docks there. Bananas, instead, were assigned to the former colonial port, which was hard to get to and surrounded by an old dead city, melted in the rain, and a cemetery white-capped with bodies. That was the banana port. The boats stayed off at a distance, as if quarantined. Banana Men were unloaded there like carriers of the plague. The banana smell stuck to their money and they were not particularly well liked in the capital. Consequently, everything their business required had been gathered together at F., nicknamed Port-Banane: big stores, banks, and brothels. It looked rather like a town in a western, minus the dust but with the rottenness, and everybody was happy.

In the port the land was invading the sea; gradually the bottom had risen. To go ashore you had to be transferred in flat-bottomed launches. Out at sea *The Will of God* resembled a glowing white tower. Advancing toward the gelatinous mountain in front of them, Victor realized that the fellow with his porthole had lied about the palm tree and about all the rest besides: the beach, the blue sky. That left only the girl in the drawing. But here she was very young with long hair ruffled by the wind, a hint of a dress, cloth sandals. It took him a long time to recognize her because he had only seen her naked.

Lola, her wicker bag on her shoulder, watched the approaching mountain. It wasn't the sun, but she thought that for her, in this country, the sun would have to be that. She was wrong about what time, what day, what year, and what continent it was. And meanwhile César, faced with the violent rot of the stinking mountain, was walking back and forth in the launch and shouting: Filth, filth! As he watched the young woman, Victor wasn't thinking about what awaited him, he was musing over the absurdity of seeing a woman naked and then encountering her with her clothes on.

Beretti stayed on the dock to supervise the unloading of the baggage. All of the boat's cargo: the stinking barrels with their sides bashed in that had to be lowered carefully, straight up and down, the enormous packing cases, burlap bags filled to bursting, the bundles. Careful! Beretti shouted, his arms raised toward all this manna, careful! And looking straight at the directors, who were still dazzled by the light and, after days spent in their rat hole, now feeling land sick because the ground refused to stabilize, you couldn't help, could you? That's all they were waiting for and they began to busy themselves on the dock like Beretti. They staggered around, waving their arms like him and shouted to the Negroes hanging onto the ropes: Careful! And to the ones loading the trucks: Gently! From the sound of things getting smashed one would be inclined to think they were irreparable. A big heap of who knows what disappeared into the sea. Thrown plumb out.

Come, said Beretti, gathering his troops together. It's not far, I'll take you. They walked along the cemetery that held whites dead of yellow fever. To express the grief, the ravages and extent of the epidemic, all anyone had been able to find were military statues: soldiers from the First World War raising bugles to their lips, women kneeling beside soldiers who were stiff or lifeless, wrathful roosters, helmeted cherubs, and all of it firmly entangled in stone drapes, shrouds with hard folds and Alsatian bowknots stiff as the cement in which they were cast. A war? Victor asked. No, replied Beretti, an epidemic. But, there being an overproduction of monuments to the dead, the tearful town councils had sold them to a grateful Africa.

They went down a dirt road with holes in it here and there, between apartment buildings from colonial days that vegetation had recaptured with a fury, secreting whatever clawlike roots, knotted branches, and poisonous thorns were required along with pillboxes more recently constructed from salvaged material, tombstones carved with the name of a few Frenchmen, bars whose age could be estimated by the layers of rust, a sort of huge dumping ground bristling with posters, crowned with neon lights, electrified to high heaven: shooting stars that would shine and then go out, cowboys formed of lightbulbs alternately flashing green then red, airplanes that took off and landed, mouths that opened and closed, blinking eyes . . . All of that in a spasmodic count of one-two, one-two, verging on short-circuit. The electricity didn't get down to where people were. Down below they were still using wood fires, stagnant water, and the mortar with its tireless pestle in the slow gestures that date from the beginning of the world. On the doors a few naïve paintings vaunted the merits of a hairdresser, a tailor, and dubious import-export establishments – dubious at least as far as spelling was concerned.

African Resource. That's it, said Beretti. They went into a huge warehouse. Roof-high in bundles precariously balanced, which the same Negroes they had seen at the docks were scaling perilously. Behind the counter: a fine young mulatto man with golden copper skin, splendid eyes, green and transparent as emeralds, fringed with thick, long, curly lashes as impressive as the stamens of certain carnivorous plants, his torso bare, already slightly plump, wearing a gold chain. So handsome that he was frightening.

Hi, Uncle. The formal embrace, backslapping on bare skin. How's Papa? Beretti asked, thus demonstrating the sacred, indissoluble, family nature of the business. Still the same. The voice came from behind the cash register. Another mulatto, a woman this time, but worn out, greenish yellow, a shriveled, distorted version of the boy. He was the flower, she the leaf, stem, or thorn. To hear her tell it, Papa had lost his wits, he couldn't stand people coming near him, he didn't want anyone to talk to him. So, now what? said the girl sulkily.

I'm going to say hello to him anyhow, said Beretti. The girl shrugged. Her shoulders were very thin. Just by her thorax, which jutted out over the counter by the cash register, you could tell she was puny and knock-kneed. The silent directors, still reeling from the voyage, stayed on the other side of the counter, the line dividing the world in two. Beretti walked over to a glass cube that rather resembled the ones in museums where ancient artifacts are kept. The master of the house, the papa of the Resource, sat enthroned inside, fantastically obese, sheltered from the noise and heat and watching the comings and goings of his business. He was in a refrigerated box. His vast flesh stuck to the glass, making pink patches adhering here and there, wherever his body touched, as if he were held inside his box by suction cups. At night two servant boys tipped it over on its back so he could sleep. He used signals to give orders, a pulley moving his right hand. He would give one look to a servant boy, who then raised or lowered the hand. He didn't want to move anymore; he didn't want to be touched.

It's me, said Beretti. Finally, said the obese man. Then, for what seemed a very long while, nothing more. The obese man, his eyes blank, was dreaming a harsh, concrete dream that wouldn't fade. They wanted to help him along. Well, so? said Beretti. Well, so? said the obese man and, scarcely moving at all though it still made the pulley squeak, he pointed to the back of the warehouse. All that . . . said Beretti, not counting what I'm bringing back. Then there was another long moment of nothing. The obese man was having difficulty getting rid of his dream, with the result that he just stared wild-eyed. You expected a hiccup or a spasm, some internal event that would release him. Victor was familiar with these long waits, these interminable greetings, the small talk masking the real questions but never anything resembling this. He thought they'd better wake him up; from one word to the next he was going to forget that they were there.

They're there, Beretti launched right in. Then, as if to excuse himself: It's all I could find. They were dirty and unshaven, only Victor had tried to get dressed and put on his black suit and a tie. A band of convicts with blazing eyes like wolves. The obese man stared at them; the sound of business woke him up. I've filled them in and they agree, said Beretti. Victor didn't dare interrupt him, surely he had to know what he was doing. For the moment he trusted Beretti. The obese man nodded his head: 50 percent paid on delivery, the rest billed for later. Yes, said Beretti. Including the stock, the obese man made clear. Obviously, said Beretti. OK, that's fine, the obese man concluded. Beretti turned to his directors and indicated that things were going well.

The fellows were waiting behind the counter as if it were the starting line. He's like that, said Beretti. When you think what a merchant he was formerly . . . The best one of us, the best of all. Started from nothing; I can't tell you what a dump it was. Not like you. You're being provided with the premises, the stock, and customers. Nothing to do. Except, yes! And here he guffawed: *sell* . . . You'll draw for who gets which branch. It was as if he were the starter and the finish line happiness. They were on the starting blocks. Behind her cash register the mulatto woman wrote down the names of the branches on bits of paper. Unknown places, unpronounceable names, but they were pleased to read the meaningless words, as if fate had favored them with what it had awarded. They had an hour.

The men scattered with the joyful frenzy of a class when school lets out. They knew where they intended to spend recess, all of them – in the brothel. Corrugated metal, cardboard, bits of wood, a palace with the architecture of a wedding cake, there was a brothel for every taste. Bonne arrivée, called the girls on the doorsteps; Welcome, they called out as they lifted the bead curtains at more modest establishments; Willkommen. They interrupted a meal of red beans and corned beef; they chased the flies away; they went straight to work. Hurry up, said the guy, his mind already somewhere else, hurry up, my truck's about to leave.

Victor had stayed behind in the warehouse. You, what are you doing here? asked Beretti, the way you ask a child who isn't playing. And like a child hanging back indoors during recess, Victor didn't answer. You're not going with the others? asked Beretti. Victor gave a faint smile that was sufficient indication that he didn't understand much about such games. Is it because of the old lady? asked Beretti.

Inside the box the pulley worked its lines and cogs and the obese man signaled them to come over; he wanted to tell them something. They went past the counter and, with great respect for the idol, surrounded the box. Victor detected something like a mouse squeak; he had never heard anyone speak through a block of glass. Papa was addressing him. He's asking your age. Twenty, Victor replied. But that didn't tell those people anything about those twenty years of the way it used to be. Twenty years cocooned and nurtured to maturity by a woman – a woman of another generation. Twenty years with the modesty of a virgin, the candor of a child, the innocence of a young girl; twenty years that brought a blush to the cheek and tears to the eye; twenty years that didn't know how to talk. The young man in black must have worn all that like a halo, or perhaps it was just his beauty, which was like a light shining from his eyes. Consultations. Whispers. I'd thought of that, replied Beretti. Papa wants to assign you to the Model Village, he said. That's César's place, a branch we take particularly good care of. Congratulations, you can write that to your grandmother. Thank you, sir, said Victor, clueless. I'm putting you in the hands of the foreman of the banana plantation, you'll be leaving shortly with the trucks from Devil's Banana. Thank you, sir, Victor said again.

Sunset Boulevard

The Sunset occupied the former governor's palace: white columns and a veranda, colonial-style with hibiscus. It might have passed for a slightly down-at-the-heels luxury hotel, and you could still make out the administration's old copper plaques through the pink paint covering the doors: Passport Office, Marriage Bureau, Registry Office. On the pediment in place of the French flag that used to wave, a blue neon sign flashed day and night. Affecting the airs of a club, the Sunset served as bar, restaurant, and hotel. A big red velvet curtain, scrapped by the theater in Limoges, hid a formal staircase in the back of the bar and marked the limits of the brothel proper – the frontier between day and night, between what was acceptable and what was forbidden. Going to the brothel always meant, more or less, going behind the curtain. One evening a month it opened theatrically on a theme party with performances. Drinks twice the price.

The owner, a former French actress now going by her first name alone, told anyone willing to listen the story of her disasters: solely to keep her from competing with their stars, the Americans had made her sign a fantabulous agreement in her glory days. The Sunset Boulevard was all she had saved of Hollywood, of the massacre of time and the forgetfulness of men. She happily showed off the press clippings telling how she was making a fresh start, how she had found happiness. Necklaces made of flowers, her face already puffy from beer and a too-young, dark-haired, Latin companion described in the article as the man who brought about her resurrection. He was the one who took her to Africa; he was the one who left her there. Meanwhile he had put out her eye.

Ysée required her girls to be white, classy, and distinguished, with false eyelashes and gowns trimmed in swansdown at the hem. A hairdresser came every morning to put their hair up in stiff black chignons resembling Iroquois headdresses, Amazon helmets. He spread vast quantities of blond hair over their shoulders, setting each curl one at a time with hairspray. Ysée herself would only appear in a hat and veil so as to hide the lifeless eye that was a milky blotch on her face. At the Sunset a Hollywood ambiance reigned, reimagined and improved by Barbie dolls, and the whole thing spiced up with a thoroughly French touch of culture.

Ysée had *tremendous ambition* for her girls, as she said. A girl with no regard for perfection, without the insatiable will to advance, to learn, was lost. Consequently, the initiation was harsh and threw some doubt on many of the clichès about the slovenliness of this sort of house where anything goes. Nothing lax about this brothel. Ysée ran her house with an iron hand, with implacable authority. The girls, conforming to the fantastic discipline of 20th Century Fox, learned to sing and dance and act. They took lessons in deportment. Ysée taught them to sit with their legs together. She showed them how to hold their purses just like the Queen of England and many, many other things necessary to life in society. She told them: You are Princesses, never forget it. Be that as it may, when cocktail hour rolled around, the Princesses rested their hairsprayed heads and their good manners against their bolsters and delivered their bodies, stripped of swansdown, to the rough assaults of the Banana Men.

As for the bar, there was the usual throng on the days that boats arrived. The inhabitants of Port-Banane, despite always hoping for fresh news, proved to be fond of news that was several weeks old and that they had already heard on the radio, because the voyagers, like survivors of catastrophe, transformed it until the news had a credibility lacked by cut-and-dried information borne by a fainter voice from the other end of the world. At the bar, just as in the office, the easiest and the most urgent business was settled first. This was the time of day when the Sunset was the City; you could only just barely make out the girls moving around behind the curtain from Limoges, the muffled sounds as they rehearsed a show, and the nasal tones of a record beating out a rhythm for their feet.

César, my darling! César, dear heart! He had just come in, this love of love. Ysée was in his arms, cooing with emotion and happiness. She was bound to César by old, unshaken ties. It was with her that his impotence had first raised its feeble head and then progressed as their firm friendship became established; in bed they spent more and more time talking business. Those were the days when she ran a sleazy dive with two girls and she had been obliged to make sacrifices. One day they realized that they were getting undressed and into bed with the exhilaration of swimmers undressing and diving in, just to talk about money. With the sheets pulled up they were chattering away like accountants. She had big dreams. He had bought her the Sunset. You see, she said to him, what you did for me, I'll be eternally grateful to you. He set up his bedroom in the old governor's office. From the terrace he could see the ocean; he contemplated the container ships full of bananas and, off in the distance, he saw The Will of God gleaming like a sun. He was at home; he brought his women there. He was the most beloved man in the world. He dreamed: When I've had enough, you see, this is where I'll retire.

At the sight of César, the drinkers at the bar sat up straighter on their seats and the girls bustled around behind the curtain. We missed you, César, said Ysée, stepping back so she could see him better. Here, said César, pushing Lola out in front of him. Oh! no, she said as she saw her. Oh! no. Exclaimed joyfully before a gift that was in very bad taste but still amusing, and he rocked back and forth there, one leg on the other and very proud of how he'd set her up . . . César, what's that you've brought! Not pretty? César wheedled. Not pretty? All black like that? And, less sure of himself now that he had seen the bananas and noticed that his foreman stood devastated and overwhelmed with shame in a corner of the room, he looked around at the people in the room and his buddies to say it was so. His joke seemed less good. Lola was like a wet fart, like a firecracker that fizzles. She's not black! said a guy at the bar. Well, what do you need? Ysée exclaimed. Not white, either, the guy added. Ah! that's better, said Ysée, you scared me, and she brought both hands up to her breast to pretend her emotion was so strong that her heart was going to come right out through her bosom.

Here, said César, stepping behind Lola, this is for you. For me! Suddenly serious again. Absolutely not! What do you want me to do with this? Girls like this, they are on every sidewalk in Mégalo; girls like this, there are plenty of them on your banana plantation. Do you realize what would have to be done to make her – I'm not even saying acceptable but just presentable. Thanks a lot, I've barely finished with the Lana Turner promotion! That's OK, that's OK; visibly annoyed, he played for time. It was a joke. I'll keep her for myself. It's not like I don't want to make you happy. César, you know perfectly well, but a girl like that is the bad seed in the bunch, mold on the jam; she'll ruin the Sunset's reputation in less than no time. I said it was OK, César interrupted, and this time he was entirely serious; she felt it and it worried her. Come, she said to Lola, we're going to leave the men to themselves. Guastavin! called César.

The foreman came over. In the old days he had been César's friend, more or less his alter ego. In business matters one name was never mentioned without the other and people pretended they never knew which was which. They had begun together,

33

but César had profited more from their conjoined existence than Guastavin. Money, happiness, women, food – he'd taken it all. The foreman was withering away; you could tell by his shoes, which got bigger and bigger. Good heavens! Guastavin, growing feet at your age! exclaimed Ysée. No, M'dame, he replied, it's that my calves are shrinking. Two strings in his ugly army boots.

César and the foreman sorted through all the ins and outs of the putrid mountain. Guastavin had done his job: he had overseen first the harvest and then the shipping of the bananas to the port. But that is where they were held up, a foreman's nightmare! You should have paid, César reproached him. But who? Pay who? Everything you were supposed to pay had been paid, and here the foreman ran through an incredible list, from ministers to orderlies. And the president? No, the foreman had not gone quite that far. He'd never even thought of the president. After all, you should have made them into something! César said, rather dishonestly, he knew perfectly well that there was nothing to be done with them other than ship them, not even can them in syrup.

. . . You're all the same, you think all you have to do is show up to be hired. You think all you have to do is come to Africa to win the jackpot. Well, I'll tell you something: Africa is just like America, damn hard. The men here have everything at their fingertips, and free. To make them pay you have to give them something deluxe, something classy, top quality. A body is nothing, everyone has two legs, two arms, and all the rest! You'll learn that a body is what's around it, how it is presented. When you no longer have hair but a coiffure, no tits or ass but a silhouette, no legs but a way of walking, no skin but a perfume, not just two eyes any more but a gaze – then, my girl, we'll discuss it. You're all the same – thinking all you have to do is lie down and open your thighs, but a man doesn't go to bed with a slit, he goes to bed with the dream you project.

34

Ysée told Lola the whole fantastic history of her life in Hollywood. To back this up she pulled out a somewhat dog-eared copy of a movie magazine as proof; leafing through it she talked about Marilyn, Jane, Carol as if they had all spent a lot of time together: her bosom buddies. She said, it's like Marilyn, how they killed her. She could never warn her girls enough against the movie world: shady lawyers, pimps, sexist directors, debauched producers. Ysée was fascinating, especially because she was reciting newspapers. You had the impression that what she said was true because she repeated word for word things you had already read, a story simultaneously fuzzy and precise, full of kind feelings and innuendos. She reawakened memories, she brought out irrefutable evidence: the suicides of Martine and Marilyn, the semiretirement of Brigitte. She confirmed how smart Michèle had been and how beautiful Marlene's legs.

Lola had the fabulous sense of being right there at the table with Ava Gardner and Audrey Hepburn all gathered within the ineffable aura of Garbo. The snow princess, the swan of Moscow! Ysée confirmed, and seeing the adoring, covetous gaze, she was suddenly gripped by an emotion that was almost artistic: Fantastic youth, she murmured. César is not reasonable. What are we going to do with you, sweetie? Lola didn't know; measuring up to Ysée's perfection, she estimated, would take a lot of doing. She bore her youth like a flaw. She felt fragile, defenseless and, above all, terribly awkward, extremely black. She implored: Someday maybe? She begged: Later? Ysée gathered the young woman's hair together in her hands and pulled it back. Lord, what a mop! But she hadn't said no.

Ysée! someone called from the back of the room. It was a small man, badly shrunken with age, whose hands were the only parts still their original size; they seemed enormous. Lola recognized the fellow who had said just now that she didn't seem too black to him; she was grateful for this and half stood to offer him her chair. You know, Ysée, about the Dame de Montsoreau. Here we go again, back to that; back to his stubborn obsession. He's been this way ever since he read the *Dame de Montsoreau*. Spent his whole life in bananas, and then one day a book; the only thing on his mind is that book. She spoke to him gently; so much age deserved respect: but what would you do with the Dame de Montsoreau?

The old man had his own idea, which he began to describe just as he had done incessantly ever since a stroke suddenly sensitized him to the pure beauty of noble and valorous sentiments. "Then she said," "then he said," "then afterward," "but meanwhile…" It infuriated Ysée. Why doesn't he bug off with his Dame de Montsoreau. And to make her opposition crystal clear: It just can't be staged. He already had his hand in his pocket to pay.

She had staged *Sissi* and *Cleopatra*, her two greatest successes, with a daring medieval fresco, after which the Banana Men could have it off with Ladies wearing pointed hats and wimples. These cinemato-historical recreations required an incredible expenditure of energy, a tireless imagination, and more than the usual financial means. Silk is silk, otherwise *you don't see silk* – that was her motto. She was always threatening that she wasn't strong enough, or brave enough anymore, but her audience wildly encouraged her; the Banana Men advanced significant subsidies. She had received Mégalo's Medal for Arts and Letters. The photo in *Le Journal* had been terrible, all ink with a white splotch in the middle, made immeasurably broader by her satisfied smile. She stopped smiling; she was past the age for that.

However, the old man said, pointing at Lola with his chin, the little one, she'd do. She's not staying here, said Ysée. Knowing now that she wouldn't be staying at the Sunset any longer, that the break was final, after having first feared then hoped to stay in such a pleasant place, Lola's heart tightened. She asked if she could take some copies of *Cinémonde* with her. Ysée loaned her the book that all the actresses used at 20th Century Fox – the book of advice and memories of a former makeup artist, Miss Priddy, the lady who had made them all blond, thin, long, glamorous, and nasty. Begin by reading this, she told her.

The Truck Race

The trucks from Devil's Banana were waiting in front of the Sunset for César to give the starting signal. Already two hours late, they wouldn't get there before dark. César helped the girl climb into the cab of the first truck and took the steering wheel himself. At that instant, all the drivers of all the trucks leapt as one into their cabs, you heard the din of a single door banging, the fantastic roar of thirty thousand horses racing in unison.

Squeezed in between the mechanic and the driver of the thirteenth truck, Victor felt the machine rattle and gather speed. In front of him the dust of twelve trucks, behind him the dust of ten trucks, on either side dust, dust. Watch out, said the mechanic, this is going to be one helluva race! And a helluva race it was, with fierce vibrations, manic accelerations, savage braking, screeching skids. The driver, very tense at first, carried out a sequence of precise and rapid moves: double-clutchings, brake-skids, stops and starts, the whole thing performed with great turns of the steering wheel, using all the strength of both arms, both biceps, to spin it. Victor took a lot of this in the ribs, particularly because every move made to manage the truck was re-created on his right side by the mechanic, who took it upon himself to repeat everything the driver did. He drove with an imaginary steering wheel, a pretend gearshift, a supposition of a brake; he amplified the sounds with his mouth – spluttering, whistling, squealing. We're off! he puffed.

Everybody knew that whenever he came back from France, César, along with his drivers, coolies, and foremen, organized a race. The point was to pass him. It was an initiation race serving to reestablish his authority and to rein in any ambitions that might have sprung up during his prolonged absence. But for the drivers it invariably revived their dreams. You should have seen the care they took, dolling up their big trucks, tuning their engines, polishing their bodies. They drove them to water holes and washed them, scraping the tires the way they would have cleaned the feet of an elephant. And then, when the truck had been well scoured, they decorated it with ribbons, paper flowers, magical inscriptions intended to guarantee success and protect them from the evil eye. *By the grace of god; a word to the wise is enough; death – who gives a fuck!*

But the one thing they did give a fuck about was the death of a truck, a truck rolled over, lying in a ditch, a truck that had crashed and burned. The driver, when he did survive, would stay by its side keeping an eye on it so no one could dismember it or carry off any parts. He watched it right up to the end, all the way to the junkyard, where he would mourn it for all eternity. The fate of those who had lost their trucks through their own fault was not pleasant; they were condemned to walk eternally behind its ghost. Sometimes you would meet up with these poor wretches and mistake them for pilgrims or madmen; it was nothing but orphaned drivers.

Victor was hurled against the windshield. The truck had braked, then stopped. The troop had come to a halt. Are we there? he asked the driver, who was wearing his eyeglasses like Papa Doc's henchmen, to show his importance as a driver. The fellow shrugged his shoulders in scorn for this white trash who didn't know how things were done. No, said the mechanic, we've only just come into the banana plantation. The settling dust let the treetops emerge with their long, rolled-up leaves erect against the sky, big leaves in a fan, turgescent flowers, green clusters, miniscule bananas rising in tiers. This is it? Victor asked. This is it, said the mechanic.

Is it big? asked Victor. The driver sneered. First there's the Devil, then the Bull, which joins the Elephant. Maybe twenty thousand acres, the assistant said, maybe more. And after that? I mean beyond that, what's there? Victor asked. The driver took his hand off the wheel and gave a wave that was at the same time far-reaching and vague. In the old days, said the assistant, there was forest. But since this information seemed to annoy the driver, he quickly added, apparently that's just a story . . . There's nowhere better than the Devil, the assistant concluded, with enough servility to please the driver. Victor wondered what they were doing there in the middle of the road.

When César entered the plantation and saw the first line of banana trees he reached the height of arousal. He loved his banana plantation; he loved everything about it, every bunch, every banana. Stopping his truck, he would drag the current Lady into the rows of banana trees for a bit of faunlike and natural merrymaking, a foretaste of *real life*. Once again he had not failed to perform this rite and was now making joyful sacrifices to the banana god Pan. In this case, he was counting on the familiarity of the place, the vibrations of the race for the event. He had pushed Lola behind the banana trees. The trucks waited.

Victor caught sight of her emerging from the banana trees; she was a good distance away. That she was along for this journey seemed to him a good omen. The convoy set off again, but slowly; they crawled along on a road of laterite through countryside of peerless monotony. The driver expressed his disappointment by banging the palm of his hand on the steering wheel. Covered with sheepskin, it was so thick that it looked more like an automobile tire. Ignoring Victor, he talked to the mechanic and together the two launched into a lot of fast talk, full of laughter.

Victor was tired, he was wondering how he was going to describe a banana tree, a banana, to his grandmother when he wrote a letter. He could still see the ones they used to buy at the grocery store. You couldn't be lyrical about them, and he felt that, to make her happy, he should tell her about something exceptional, incredible, and beautiful. Had it been any other tree he would have slipped a leaf or a petal in with the letter. He wondered if his grandmother had ever told him any stories that had banana trees in them. Couldn't remember. His only inspiration was what he knew, not what he would discover, except for the girl . . . but, in some ways, he did know her.

Suddenly night fell. The headlights revived the dusty green of the leaves. You could see just about as well as before. It was only the light from the invisible sky that had vanished. Victor was relieved to see a few houses indicating they were near a village, cabins along the edge of the road that were built of clay and straw mortar mixed with the very dust of the road. The big refrigerated trucks shook them as they went by. So, are we there? Victor asked, restless and stubborn the way children are who don't dare say they're tired. We're going to the garage, said the assistant driver proudly, because he knew he would be performing the most important part of his job – minding the truck overnight, and, if the driver was in a good mood, cleaning it, scrubbing the tires and getting between their deep ridges to dislodge the mud, hosing down the truck body, maybe opening the hood and sticking his head inside to breathe in the engine's hot, oily smell. He was humbly awaiting a glance from behind the driver's dark glasses. But the driver was still not sure whether he was happy or unhappy about the race. There were arguments on both sides. He hadn't won, but he hadn't lost. He had kept his position through several skillful swerves right and left that had kept the others from passing him. But he hadn't done better than they had, and that was what Mister César would tell them; so maybe, feeling humiliated, he would want to lie down next to the big truck and watch the stars come up as he waited for the heat of the race to vanish like the fever on a sick child's forehead.

The trucks lined up parallel to each other on a broad esplanade surrounded by garages and gas pumps. César began to speak. Victor vaguely understood that it was not yet the moment for the owner of the Devil to be surpassed as driver: he had found them much more chicken than the last time, and then he lit into the one who was last. To Victor's surprise he saw that it was a white man, a slovenly sort, tense and tired, who did not seem to have enjoyed the race. So Guastavin, always lagging behind? Do you think you're on your tractor? And the drivers, who a moment earlier were feeling hurt, felt a good deal better seeing the one who came in last be mocked; though he couldn't have been anything but last, since that was his starting position and he had been given the assignment to bring up the rear. That was one of the niceties of the way César exercised power: proclaiming himself the winner and, so this wouldn't be too unbearable, designating the loser.

Victor saw the girl again; she was climbing into a jeep where César took the steering wheel. He didn't really recognize her in the light from the headlights; her hair was up. For the first time he saw the contours of her face. The innocence of her neck and freshness of her cheeks moved him. If you want to go with Mister Guastavin, said the assistant, he's over there, and Victor hurried over to the downcast white man, who had climbed up onto a tractor. Victor hoisted himself onto the rounded fender covering a huge wheel and the coolies crammed themselves into a trailer. There was no one wearing glasses there and no assistant driver, either. The drivers aren't coming? Victor asked. No, Guastavin replied, they are going home, to the real village; as for us, no such luck, we have to go all the way to the Model Village. Victor understood that employees were divided into two categories: the ones who had the right to live the way they liked (from whom the drivers were recruited) and the poor wretches, runaways, displaced ones who lived according to the rules of the Model Village and took care of the dirty work. Victor felt that he had crossed the line where the waters parted, the line dividing the world, and that the tractor was slowly but inexorably taking him toward the down-and-outs, the dropouts, the lower-than-the-low.

They stopped at the entrance to a group of huts where, night and day, the powerful generators providing refrigeration for the bananas supplied streetlamps as tall as watchtowers with a blue-white light. Victor, in his black wool suit, was as hot and tired as he could be, but more than that, he had an indefinable and suffocating sense of discomfort; he was short of breath. Beneath the blue light, on either side of a straight road hermetically sealed shacks enclosed the bit of darkness required for sleep. The day was outside, the night inside. You could see pieces of paper flying about; you could distinguish the red glow of the eye of a cat, its ghost decomposed by the violent, crackling light.

Guastavin

They zigzagged through a shack with all the defenses of a small fort. Victor heard chains clanking but mostly what he heard were groans and sighs, the sounds of exertion, in Guastavin's throat and chest. Guastavin loosened shutters, drew bars, rolled barrels of sand out of the way. He cleared an opening in the wall. With a quick gesture of command, the kind they say officers make when they give the order to attack, he signaled Victor to follow him.

They entered a dark airlock. Without a word and scrupulously following a checklist, Guastavin began the painstaking reconstruction of the defenses behind Victor. When everything was locked up tight, he used a key to open a door that Victor had not noticed at the far end of the hole. A very crude, very white lamp lit a living room with two black plastic armchairs, a low table, straight chairs lined up along the wall and, in the back of the room, next to a refrigerator, a large abstract picture, a tortuous and aggressive pencil drawing.

Guastavin sprawled breathless in an armchair, his arms dangling. S'down, he said to Victor, Make y'self t'ome. Victor took off his black jacket; it was hot and damp and beneath it his torso was streaming. The foreman got even further undressed, naked now except for a pair of saggy briefs serving as a loincloth and his stiff leather clodhoppers, which he had untied. S'down, he repeated, pointing to an armchair and shouting something at it. Victor almost jumped out of his skin when a black shape broke away from the plastic. A silhouette dwarf and long at the same time, a small, not at all human human. Victor had never seen a chimpanzee.

With a great sweeping gesture the creature quickly picked up the foreman's scattered clothes and, in the same swoop, attempted to grab the black jacket, which Victor defended by hugging it to his chest. Thwarted, the monkey backed away, walking like a spider. It took the clothes under one arm and stuck them in a half barrel that was used as a laundry tub and sink. She's going to clean them, the foreman explained, showing a certain satisfaction for the first time, the sort a fellow might feel at home, where all he has to do is put his feet under the table. Bring us something to drink! Guastavin shouted. The monkey, halfway in the barrel, turned a deaf ear. Apparently it didn't like being bothered when it was busy, and besides, it seemed to like the spurting water and abundant soapsuds. Something to drink! shouted Guastavin.

Reluctantly, the chimpanzee went over to the refrigerator, opened it, took out a six-pack of beer, which it placed on the table and, still grudgingly, unearthed some salted almonds from a cupboard. At a snail's pace it carried them over, hesitated an instant as to whether or not it would keep them, and then, at the foreman's curt and guttural command, flung them on the table. It pulled a chair up to the table, climbed onto it, and began to scratch its neck and back with one of its upper hands and somewhere in the vicinity of its groin with a lower one. Guastavin handed a can of beer to Victor and one to the monkey; they opened them and lifted the beer to their lips.

Welcome, said the foreman in English, raising the hand holding the beer can in salute. That's how they say it here: Welcome. But there was nothing happy about the way he said it. Victor felt himself falling into the depths of darkness – the last in a sequence of falls: from the little village to Bordeaux, from Bordeaux into the bowels of *The Will of God*, from the boat's hold to the docks at Port-Banane, from Port-Banane to this nameless village, into this final dark hole that was Guastavin's dingy living room, into something bordering on despair. It was too far, too deep, it would take too much effort, too much time to climb back up the slope; already you couldn't see daylight where they were. He understood what they were talking about in church when they said eternity.

And yet he heard himself talking with an uncalled-for confidence (made even more ridiculous, indeed illusory by how deeply exhausted the foreman looked) about how he was there on a commercial venture, to "develop," as Monsieur Beretti put it, "the African resource." He said, just to say them, the words that had reassured him and that no doubt continued to delight his grandmother; he hung onto them like a piece of rope. Between him and the nightmare there was only the transparent layer of formal address – the way he said the formal "you," the "Monsieur" lightly

44

spoken before all names as he had been taught. But he already knew that his story didn't stand up and there was no sense laying it on for this man across from him. This man understood the whole works: from the first field with the first banana tree, which he himself had put in the ground, from the first coolie he had hired, from the first cinderblock, even in some ways from the first stone. And for proof? All he had left were amputated words, words with first their civility and then their sense cut off, monkey language.

You can't tell it now but in the old days, yes, in the old days, it all worked fine. He and César were like the fingers of a hand, and then, nobody knew why, but the same as twins, one had grown larger at the expense of the other. He'd been so pleased with César's success that it took Guastavin a long time to understand that this success was at great cost to himself. When he did notice it was too late. He had lost his position and was condemned to run far behind César. The most hated because the most beloved. Normal.

No one knows how, but even in everyday life and between the most ordinary people there are turnarounds that are almost political, alliances reversed, sudden breakups, secret agreements; there are defeats, retreats, routs like on the most heroic battlefields, and there are some disasters that bleed you more bloodless than a thousand deaths. Who says life is monotonous, that nothing happens? Not here, anyhow. With grand strategies you went from one battle to the next, from one body to the next, you were the general and the cannon fodder, the victory and the defeat. And for no good reason: it might depend on a woman walking by, some encounter, some unspeakable feeling, a storm that doesn't break and one word too many. And then the thing you'd counted on most – pfft! Screwed, washed up, trashed. T'day, as he said, what Victor saw was a man exiled from exile.

He'd felt things weren't going well; he could easily see that César no longer liked him or at least didn't like him as much as before. He mentioned it to him. César indignantly exclaimed: How can you say that! And then, friendship this, friendship that, assuring him of all the friendship in the world. Friends, not brothers . . . But still, it was something. And then no more friendship, and Guastavin was back on the attack. He was the one speaking in the name of friendship, saying that very cold though neutral word. And César had replied that friendship wasn't the only thing in life, that besides it was no excuse, friendship couldn't make one blind . . . One day (the foreman could have told you the hour and the minute) he no longer called him by his name and nicknamed him "Guastavino" . . . And I don't drink! Now there was nobody who remembered his real identity; he himself pretended to have forgotten it . . . Only César, perhaps (and it was his only hope) remembered it guiltily, conscious of his crime. He was telling Victor this to make him understand that he was not good company the way a certain "Mister" Gilbert, who thought he was so important, was . . . He was full of bitterness, drowning in resentment.

The monkey displayed utter boredom interrupted by monotonous scratching. It scratched itself lethargically, for no particular reason, with a long bony index finger. Victor was getting used to this rubbery face with its heavily engraved features, carved with a knife, you'd say – deep mouth wrinkles, two nostrils. He didn't think it very handsome. He looked at the dense, black body hair, all bushy around its neck. He couldn't keep his eyes off the hands; it bothered him that the creature had four of them, all moving at once, endlessly busy and unpredictable. One day, said the foreman, somebody brings you a baby, no bigger than a cat, sweet and gentle, and in less time than it takes to tell it, the animal weighs a hundred pounds, it turns into a schmuck, it balks, it's lazy, dirtier than you can imagine, fierce and lecherous; but what do you want, he said with a sweet look on his face, it's too late; you're attached. The monkey was so affected by this attachment that she helped herself to another beer without Guastavin so much as thinking of preventing her.

She's bored, said Guastavin. And you have to understand her, she never goes out, just does a little housework, a little cooking but she doesn't have many distractions. I can't take her with me to the plantation; they want to take her away from me. They say I have no right to keep her; they think she's some sort of spell-bound human, bewitched. Their only thought is to make her go away, and as for her that's all she ever thinks of, too. They were almost successful three months ago, but the drivers brought her back to me. She was wandering around near the cabins. She must have met up with a troop of chimpanzees but hadn't been able to follow them. No more strength in her arms. Now, when I come home at night, I'm always afraid I won't find her here. She's cunning; she has watched me for a long time and knows how I lock up. When she left me I thought I would go mad. In the end I got her back – in this state. She's pregnant, said the foreman, and since Victor remained stonily indifferent, *She won a little jackpot*. The monkey understood; she made a little sound, a chuckle, she had raised her lips and, showing all her teeth, was expressing the most extreme carnivorous satisfaction. Victor noticed then that her belly stuck out and her breasts were swollen. He had never seen a pregnant woman; his first sight of maternity came with this nacreous belly covered in long black hairs. He realized that the monkey was naked. He was dreadfully ill at ease, not that he thought that Guastavin and the monkey might have . . . but really, the pregnancy had suddenly made her strangely sexual. From behind her half-lowered eyelids she stole a dreamy glance in Victor's direction. She touched him lightly, almost mechanically with the tip of one of her lower hands. She likes you a lot, Guastavin re-

47

marked. I'm going, said Victor, standing up. Too late, said Guastavin, you have to wait until morning. Nobody goes out at night here. Why? asked Victor. The village seemed peaceful to him. Do you believe in evil? the foreman asked, thrusting his face forward. Victor believed in injustice, in trouble, he believed in the spitefulness of men, yes, of course. No, not that, said the foreman, the other kind, I can't think of the word, you know, Evil Evil! Well, there are frightening powers here, and he spoke each syllable separately: terrifying dark powers. But he already knew that Victor wouldn't believe this any more than he had believed what the boy had said about commerce. Why do you think I live this way? For fear of thieves? What would they steal? For fear of murderers? Well, let me tell you, I'd rather be dead than put up with what I endure. And if it were not for her, he said, pointing to the monkey . . . He meant Victor to understand that he would be done with it. He put two fingers in his mouth as if they were the barrel of a revolver; he pulled the trigger – one last jerk. The monkey burst out laughing.

Too late, evil was lurking and, in fact, now that he had said this, Victor heard a sort of rustling against the walls, something caressing the whole house. They're looking for an opening, said the foreman. The monkey had climbed up on her master's knees. But who are they? asked Victor. Everybody, replied the foreman, absolutely everybody. Animals, things, everything that doesn't agree, everything that rebels. He pushed his head closer as if to tell a secret. They have a religion, like a sect; they believe in a return to paradise, except for them it's a return to the country where they were born or something like that. He was talking about the entire population; he waved his hand in a way that meant things could go bad just like that. You weren't safe here the way the people at César's were. He was safe there, on open ground. And then, while he was at it, he claimed the children were implicated as well . . .

48

Children. Victor thought that was ridiculous; he was convinced that if there's anybody you can't accuse of anything, it's children – the innocence of the world. Not these, said Guastavin. Not these. According to him, the hatred the children vowed him had reached its peak. For years they had been setting traps for him. He had found fire-hardened darts in front of the house; they had installed a system of slipknots meant to strangle him; they had also tried to slip the infamous banana-snake with its deadly bite through a hole in the door. Guastavin had come through it all, emerging with increased stature and strengthened by these murder attempts. He was indestructible. And that, in fact, was exactly what made them so desperate, drove them to the breaking point. Their hours were numbered. Childhood didn't last here. Other children believed themselves eternal or immortal, but these knew they didn't have much longer. Soon they would have ant bumps popping out on their heads, and their lives, their pleasure, their happiness would be put to sleep. The fact that childhood was so short in this part of the world was basically what had saved his life. When he looked into the vicious eyes of a kid, he reassured himself by thinking that it wouldn't last. In a year or two he would bring the kid into line, dazed and submissive. The only thing left to fear was that they'd go nuts in one of those fits of murderous madness caused by their only partially extinguished childhood suddenly catching fire.

He's crazy, thought Victor, confronted with this flood of wrong accusation and taking comfort in the thought that the madness of the world resided inside the head of just this one. He's crazy, Victor reassured himself the way you tell yourself: This is just a dream. Tomorrow I'll wake up. The monkey, one arm hooked over Guastavin's shoulder, its head on his naked chest, had gone to sleep. Victor thought the sight of the man's pale, naked body touching the dark hairs of the animal was disgusting. He thought the way they were entwined was the height of indecency. The monkey turned around and lay there with its chin sagging and then, while Victor watched, its eyes opened – yellow, staring, perfectly awake. He realized that she saw him, that she even had some notion of him, that maybe she was carefully working out a plan. To get away from the monkey, Victor stared at the wall, the same way animals turn their eyes away from a human gaze; he tried to make some sense of the convolutions of the drawing that hung there.

Do you like weather reports? Guastavin asked. *Like!* The weather reports Victor knew about were the ordinary farmers' signs: a cat using its paw to wash behind its ear, the nervous energy in a mane at the approach of a thunderstorm, and the way dogs doze off on the hearth when snow is falling. But here . . . I listen to the marine forecast, the foreman explained, and he recited in a dreamy voice: Dogger Bank, Fisher Bank . . . Weather is warfare, he said. I draw the paths of hurricanes, I predict the battles in the sky, and sometimes I lose track of high-pressure systems. You ought to get interested in it. Because here, he added, what we have the least of is weather. Weather, he repeated in English, to make his point. They had stretched out in their armchairs a bit and closed their eyes; light blazed through their eyelids. On the verge of dreaming Victor felt overtaken by sleep and he shook himself awake, letting out a flood of words: Was there a summer? A winter? He'd heard tell of a dry season and a rainy season. In the old days, yes. Guastavin had been through terrible tornados, endless rains that dissolved the earth into torrents of mud, black skies in the middle of the day, a sun so fiery that it dried up all the water right down to the last drop; that was the last thing the last man had remembered . . . but now, the plantations in areas like these had upset everything. The clouds had fled the sky, giant sprinklers had replaced rain. Every day, I'm telling you the truth, every

50

single God-given day you are going to hear sprinklers, and you're going to forget even the names of the seasons. He uttered a great sob.

The Banana Plantation

The rooster crowed: a great flaunting of noise that set his comb ablaze and fired up his red tail and two long yellow legs with quite enough wrath and impatience to spark off a day. But it was a call that had no echo; it didn't reverberate from one place to another to waken the fields, the hills, the earth, and the sky. It was this silence that woke Victor up.

The monkey was bustling about; she clanked utensils and rolled the bowls around. She set the table in a vague attempt at breakfast. What she really wanted to do was light the fire. She dove at a box of matches but Guastavin snatched it from her hands. She whined and sidled off on all fours, walking sideways and somewhat askew like a left-handed spider. Seeing her transformed into an enormous insect when he had, just a few minutes before, seen her standing upright attending to the housework, terrified Victor as a reminder of the narrow band separating the darkest of animal nature, insects that is, from what we call human.

The water was hot. Guastavin poked two holes in a can of condensed milk. The monkey insisted on pouring the Nescafé into their bowls. She put in too much. But Victor said nothing so he wouldn't have to see her revert to that black, shrunken, animal bearing that she put on when dismayed over having done something wrong. We have to go, said Guastavin. He stood up, opened a drawer, and attached a revolver to his belt. The monkey moaned. She liked to welcome him and wash his rags, also serve him something to drink as long as he was alone, but she hated to see him leave. In the evening the things she did for him made him stay; in the morning they sent him off. She liked to serve coffee; she hated the coffee that chased him away. At the first word he said she cried. With the same mouth he said hello and he said good-bye. With the same hand he would caress her and he would beat her. She loved his mouth; she loved his hand. When she has a baby she'll have something to do. The monkey looked at his mouth and cried some more. We have to go, he said, *go*! and the sound his mouth made was a moan like the one the monkey made.

The tractors and trucks from the Devil's Banana got on the road at four in the morning. It would take another two hours before the workers were finally delivered to the meeting place from which the various cutting teams were dispatched. Hardly had they climbed down from the trucks before the men set off single file beneath the banana trees to the most distant sections where they would begin. The man in charge, identifiable by his dark glasses, assessed the bunches and gave the order to cut. The man cutting raised his machete, the coolie slowed the falling hand of bananas, balanced it on his shoulder, and swayed off with it, at a quick, jerky pace, toward the truck. He barely missed colliding along the way with coolies running back to where the bananas were cut. It was a close-linked chain that they had better not break. One injury, one fall, and the entire column would have scattered, wandering off among the banana trees, suddenly panicked, spluttering words, disconcerted, disorganized, and more than that: completely disoriented.

There was nothing finer than straight lines, rectilinear lines rhythmically crossing the plantation at a constant pace. The men in charge saw to it, forever scolding, forever yelling faster, quick (in banana English it sounded shorter, more bracing, a parrot's cry). Kik, kik, the coolies chanted to keep their spirits up in the forest of bananas. Kik, the fellows coming back empty-handed told them, kik. A race against time, against the bananas' going soft, getting yellow, rotting. Kik, if you didn't want to have it all squashed when you got there. KIK-KIK-KIK, the entire banana plantation cackled away like a cloud of cockatoos.

Guastavin waited at the meeting place. All the exertion, all the bananas converged in his direction. His work consisted of lying in wait for the rising and falling columns that extended radially into the plantation, keeping an eye on everybody, watching closely for any possible breakdown, straightening someone's shoulder when its tilt might let the hand of bananas slide off. Worrying about fatigue possibly jeopardizing the rhythm, not letting them take a breath after the final exertion of heaving the bunch, overseeing how the bananas were packed on the truck, sending that one off quick as a flash, bringing the next one in, avoiding discouraging delays. Because though these guys were really up to it, and Guastavin recognized their willpower, they would refuse to carry a bunch of bananas one minute longer, or rather, they wouldn't carry it unless they were moving. Their job was to start running the instant they felt the weight on their backs and to stop when they couldn't feel it any more. That's all they wanted to do and if asked to do anything else they groused and complained. Hence the revolver.

Guastavin saw to it that the work went off without a hitch. He planned the cutting with great care; he went off reconnoitering to establish boundaries for the harvesting; with his machete he cut a marker, chopping through a banana tree with one swipe and dropping it to the ground. Once he had traced where the teams were to go he was satisfied. Ten or twenty teams, with each team responsible for three kilometers, made it a minimum of thirty boundaries he had to set on foot, plus he had who knows how many banana trees on his hands, but this was absolutely essential to having the work go well. He had had the idea of making them start out at the far end because, as they became more and more tired, the guys would be coming closer and in one last gasp the final hand of bananas, the one that was right next to the trucks, would be cut off and all they had to do was stagger over and hoist it into the trailer. They were obliged to stop so they could go home.

In the past he had organized harvesting competitions to make César happy. For prizes he awarded cans of condensed milk and those who were most deserving would be decorated: a green and yellow ribbon, a sort of Order of the Banana, which had never really caught on. He had tried to find some manly song for them to sing in rhythm to their work, something he could hear from his command car, a double-quick tune to accompany their pace, but the teams couldn't synchronize, so it was like a badly sung round when one guy hits a false note or jumps into his neighbor's part. It was discouraging. Silence was better, the requisite moans and panting along with, from time to time, the scream of one of the cutters cut, one of the coolies fired. Guastavin was a reliable man, an orderly man. All that reliability and order went to his head and he felt he could never do enough. He had real attacks of despair because days were only twenty-four hours long, because the coolies had only two arms and two legs. When one of the guys got hurt he would first complain of sabotage and then fix him as fast as possible.

Nobody rebelled against this stupid fruit, this anarchy of fertility, this eternally glutted nature that constantly had to be relieved, this inexhaustible organization, this damp, suffering fecundity, this tree left behind by the ages with neither the wood nor the branches of a tree, and this terrifying thing extended over thousands of acres, millions and millions of individuals. Suffering, exhaustion, sleepless nights, and surveys on foot did not result in hatred or repugnance for bananas – instead, the result was an irreparable hatred of man for man. Guastavin denounced the coolies and the coolies accused Guastavin of every evil. It did not take long before all the workers in the banana plantation, from the least of them to the most important, considered the foreman their sole enemy, the man who imposed a hellish pace, the man who measured the extent of land to be harvested, the man who set the schedule, the man who distributed their salaries and above all the horrendous fines and deductions. The one who waved his revolver around over the slightest thing. Hatred took the place of a lot of things; it paid off a lot better than manly songs in terms of effort and was also lots more effective than a yellow and green ribbon. It made do with KIK, KIK, and turned there for new material. It was hatred that made them work. The cutters kept at it only because they imagined that it was the foreman's neck they were cutting; the carriers carried foremen's bodies by the thousands. It was always a nasty surprise to them that, after having murdered him so many times, they would find him there like a ghost in the midst of the trucks.

Luckily for Guastavin agronomic technology accomplished a multitude of things. An insecticide plane salted the plantation down three times a week. The effect of breathing insecticide all day long made the coolies ten times more exhausted. By evening some of them, the oldest or weakest, were deeply, profoundly intoxicated. They were no longer so absolutely determined to execute the foreman and certainly not well coordinated enough to do it. At nightfall you could hear the paradoxical laughter of poisoned coolies coming from the trucks returning to the village.

But it was in the village, in the peaceful daytime activities, that hostility toward Guastavin really increased in scale. It had spread among the women workers who went off to the banana-drying plant. Workers of the first category peeled; workers who achieved second category (only after five years of peeling) sliced. They used small knives that were pointed and sharp, knives that they were supposed to put back on the racks at night. The little round slices of banana went into large autoclaves expelling a thick steam that came back out all the openings as if fresh bananas sucked it up again.

Hatred for the foreman was passed on, above all, to the children for whom the threat of Guastavin – his anger, his livid cheeks, his swollen neck – was raised with every scolding. Guastavin's pistol – bang-bang – then you'll be laid out flat with your arms crossed on your breast. They were charming, lively children but at puberty they grew two large lumps on their foreheads, their jaws slung forward, growth stopped, and then thick body hair sprouted on their spindly bandy legs. They quit school; the girls joined the drying crews and the boys, with equal enthusiasm, went to work on the banana plantation. From the moment they stopped being children they became ageless. Old people, whether middle-aged or in their youth, they formed a sad, gray mass around their offspring.

A teacher recruited and paid for by the Devil's Banana provided a fanciful schooling that was intended more as babysitting than to teach them anything. Clément was one of those people called banana-teachers here, fellows who were self-made and, since he had read some things in the dictionary, self-taught. No matter what he did he was always frustrated about the children's future. He taught reading and writing to people who didn't even know how to speak. Instruction wavered between a futile present and an absent future. The grammar exercise consisted of putting the present into the future. When the pupils had done a good job of declining the future all they had to do was recover the present.

At recess they formed gangs in the deserted village; they devised little wooden or wire rifles; they played bang-bang you're dead or hot-bat. They prowled around Guastavin's house. They climbed on it, they surrounded the house. And then, at the sound of the trucks bringing the men back and the whistle setting free the women, they took off like a flock of starlings. Their parents found them sitting on the doorstep going over their lessons, reciting the future.

The men came back. Drunk. They had a hard time walking straight; whirling their arms spread wide they stumbled and fell, waving their arms and legs, a grin on their faces. It was a horrible, humiliating spectacle. It was not a good drunkenness; it had nothing to do with wine or alcohol or drugs. It was the insecticide. Intoxicated from their work, from effort, from fatigue, they weren't coming out of a cabaret but from the banana plantation and their uncontrolled movements were the spasms of dying insects.

If they had coughed or spit they would have been pitiful, but there, with their empty heads swimming, their bloodshot eyes, their fits of dizziness, they were grotesque and disgusting. Clément had made the children believe in the dignity of work, but it was all he could do to keep them from making fun of their fathers. And the women's reaction said a lot about the effect their husbands produced in them. Silent, looking as stern as someone about to deliver a reprimand, they filled large jars with water and poured them on the men's heads to sober them up. Then, their skulls pounding with migraines, the men went back to being human again.

At night the village closed up silently around its accumulated suffering and hatred. The women put their arms around their husbands' bodies to hold onto them; they put their arms around their children's bodies to keep them from doing something wrong. Behind his back Guastavin could feel it all; fear had taken on dizzying proportions over the years. Then he set up his barrier course and wove it with wire. It was a futile battle. He knew he was protecting his life but his soul had been killed so many times it had vanished. It's *la perdida*, he said, and he was somewhat comforted that he had given this nameless thing a name.

At African Resource

The little houses of the village were divided along two roads intersecting at right angles: a cube of cement, a square of laterite, hollow tile blocks, tin, a door, a window. You could see that the architect had used graph paper from a school notebook. He had followed the thick lines for the main roads and contented himself with outlining squares for the houses. His rigorous conception presented no difficulty to the builders: He tore the page off and the workers transferred onto the ground what they saw on there; since all they had to use were prefabricated materials, all of them square, rectangular, or cubes, putting the jigsaw puzzle together wasn't hard at all. The employees at Devil's Banana couldn't get over it when they saw the thing go up in less than a week. They gave the cubes numbers.

The village was never baptized. It deteriorated so rapidly that it merely retained its paper name, and already the Model Village conceived of by César (inspired and directed by Ysée of the Sunset) had ceased to recall the perfect, geometrical working sketch that he had drawn. Its happy occupants had embellished it to their taste with old tires and buckets with holes in them, as well as, following Guastavin's model, a great deal of barbed wire fencing arranged in portcullis grills around their cheery abodes. African Resource had recently gotten a terrific bargain on the barbed wire; everything the men earned went into it. They knotted it, straggled it up and down, made it into garlands and bows and coils, and ran it through with ribbons. It was wild. When an animal would die in the barbs you couldn't get it out. Cats, despite their cunning, were its main victims. Beneath the smell of banana the village reeked of carrion, with a bit of household rot in the background.

Ysée, the organizational expert, was completely undone when she saw the garbage they poured out their one window. Any void would do; the window for them was a hole. They used it like a garbage chute. Throw it out and forget it as if, on the other side, the growing pile no longer was garbage. And in a certain sense, whether Ysée liked it or not, it wasn't. When it came time to eat you could see hands come out the window to pick a nice red tomato or a good little hot pepper right off the pile and then the same hands reappear to throw away the seeds or the stalk. You could find broken glass bottles in it, or crushed cans or chicken guts, but also manioc, sweet potatoes, squash. It's my pantry, one of the matrons joked, watching her pile grow higher.

The village terminated at African Resource; it stood at the end of the road, next to the parking lot and not far from the drying plant and the generator. In its form, appearance, and majesty the establishment resembled a warehouse, with gray cement walls and shutters of corrugated tin that was rusted right through. Victor dragged himself there; he had had no idea how hard it would be to walk in this humidity. He was burning up in his black suit in all this heat. Done in by anxiety and fatigue after the night he'd spent at Guastavin's, he was having a hard time breathing. A few more yards, just three steps, some sort of entranceway and in it a tower, a gigantic woman, six feet six inches tall and equally wide, the whole thing topped off with an entire sheet worn as a turban. Hands on her hips, she was barring the access to African Resource; next to her on her right was a humpbacked man and on her left a cripple whose leg (about as thick as a baguette of bread) met his hip at a strange angle. So? said the giant woman.

Queen Mab kept shop right in the entranceway to African Resource, beneath the overhanging tin roof that provided her with shade and beneath the prestigious sign adorning the pediment of the Port-Banane store and all the other branches. She had small things for sale: rice, noodles, lentils; she broke the chocolate into squares and sold flour by the spoonful, beans by the piece. She sold infinitesimal things: rice by the grain, a thimbleful of salt. She had set up her minuscule commerce in a store about the size of a case of soap. She marketed sugar cubes as well as a few dried chameleons and termites in a liquorish box (termites being priceless in a country where insecticide had destroyed everything). She really had the know-how. You should see the skill with which she measured and folded the pinch of something into a bit of paper, then removed a pinch of the pinch; her lofty scorn when confronted with beggars; the way she collected the money. No credit. The First Lady was born to do business. And she had to be dislodged.

With somewhat less conviction than he had demonstrated the night before when talking to Guastavin, Victor explained that he had just taken over the management of African Resource. Queen Mab frightened him. He instinctively feared old women, their self-assurance, their strength, and their freedom with language. Specifically, they displayed a familiarity with sexual matters, like indiscreet mothers talking about their children's bodies. Liberated from desire – at least so he thought – they discussed it in crude, offensive terms with the express intent of shocking, their gaze full of insinuation . . . You felt taken down a notch from your real value, your real stature. As far as women were concerned, he preferred young girls, who were less sure of themselves, a bit hesitant, unconscious of their charm or obsessively uneasy themselves so that they would never have considered appraising someone else. Like the girl from the boat had seemed, maybe . . .

I have a contract. He dug around in his pocket to show her Beretti's paper. He pointed: It's written here. Between her lids, through oblique, minuscule slits in the middle of this mass she watched him. She seemed unshakeable. She refused to take the sheet of paper. Victor felt weak and ridiculous waving his document in front of this mountain of flesh; he ventured the assumption that she didn't know how to read. Men write when they have lost *speech*, she told him: Take it however you want. I can read better than you can, she added, because I know how to read *writing*. And then she gave the two cripples an order; they removed all the stuff and put the soap box onto the sidewalk directly opposite the store. Queen Mab turned on her heels. He had offended Dignity, wounded Tradition, injured Commerce. Competition promised to be fearsome.

Victor stayed behind with the two cripples. Boss, Boss, they moaned, that's a bad woman . . . It was easy to believe them because they were so deformed. Prince Charming showed through all that unsightliness. The spell just needed to be broken. It didn't take Victor long, however, to learn that they were just victims of the banana: there was something Lilliputian about them because of their disability, along with the relentless determination associated with people who have struggled a lot and pulled through; plus they were baleful and spiteful when faced with anything that might thwart them. Boss, Boss, they said. *She* wanted the store. They had stood firm, they had defended African Resource every step of the way; Victor had arrived in the nick of time, she was in the process of taking the key. They raised the metal shutter: eighteen hundred square feet of echoing emptiness.

With its long wooden counters keeping the public away from the stock, African Resource looked a lot the way you might imagine a prison canteen. Not many things and utilitarian objects elevated to the rank of luxury items. A bar of Palmolive on its own shelf like a flacon of Guerlain and a box of Kerbronec sardines displayed as if it were blue caviar from Petrossian. Do we sell these? Victor asked. No, the assistants replied. We keep them. And that? asked Victor, pointing to steel drums with rings around them like the ones The Will of God had unloaded at Port-Banane. Them either, replied the assistants, we haven't opened them. Ah! said Victor. He looked outside and ran his gaze all the way down the road to the very end of the village: not even a cat. So there's nobody? Victor asked. Nobody, replied the assistants.

Victor's gaze went from the metal barrels glowing in the shadows at the back of the warehouse to Queen Mab sitting motionless in the sun. He blinked his eyes, turning them from shadow to light, from light to shadow, like a divining rod gone crazy over a spring it has identified without seeing it. From the barrels to the woman from the woman to the barrels as if they were part of the same riddle he couldn't solve. Queen Mab had withdrawn into her veils; her black face sparkled like coal. Everything shone, her silk dress and her gold bracelets, the silver earrings dangling from her ears. She was a living star, a ball of fire that had rolled here, petrified lightning, incandescent lava. But what does she want? Victor asked. She was waiting: it was the day that stock came in.

He resurfaced. He knew perfectly well that fate would not abandon him between three barrels and two cans of food. They watched and waited. At the end of the day he saw the line of coolies coming back from the fields one after the other and he saw the truck that delivered to the branches of African Resource. Clients and merchandise. He thanked his lucky stars. Following time-tested procedure, the truck stopped, Victor signed an invoice, two coolies unloaded while the assistants held forth. Then the driver held out his hand; Victor shook it. The driver looked at his hand; he didn't understand. Victor wondered if, perhaps, he'd made a faux pas. You have to pay, said the driver. Pay what? asked Victor.

Pay what's written there, the driver demanded. Feverishly Victor flipped through the invoice: 50 percent on delivery, the rest at the end of the month. He understood what the contract meant; he didn't contest it, but he had no money. I have to take back the merchandise, said the driver, and the coolies already seemed to be putting the packages back on the truck. Wait, wait, begged Victor, and he looked around. He thought of Guastavin. Take this, said Queen Mab; she stuffed a ball of crumpled bills into his hand. Take it. You'll pay me back later. Thank you, thank you; he held the money out to the driver. See you next week, shouted the driver. See you next week, Victor shouted gratefully and he went to unpack. What's there? asked Queen Mab. In the first batch there were toasters, in the second more toasters and in the third tins of La Lune brand wax. Victor dashed to the door. He wanted to shout: Help! The dust raised by the truck had not yet settled.

What the former director of African Resource in Model Village could have told him was that the store did not, as you might have expected, obey the laws of supply and demand; it depended entirely on the stock it was sent. Mainland France, and the whole rest of the world as well, unloaded their manufacturing mistakes onto Mégalo. And Mégalo, after having skimmed off what seemed the best, dumped the rest on Port-Banane, then Port-Banane did its own backassed choosing to make sure that the Model Village got its weekly share of rejects. The things they'd seen go by! Irregulars, insane contraptions, odd gadgets, nightmarish good ideas, not counting the relics of past fashions, colors that didn't catch on, obsolete shapes, banned material, inflammable toys, irradiated milk.

It all came in ridiculous quantities, a truckload of carcinogenic undershirts for babies, a crate of large-toothed metal zippers that had briefly been the equipment of choice for men's flies but were now already rusty, a truckload of bluing to whiten whites, a truckload of something red to whiten teeth. Here people had to make do with the abundance they were sent. The natives applied the same instinct their ancestors had used to elude traps in their original forest to discover the ones set for them by the West.

The fate of a stock was played out in an afternoon; it depended in part on Queen Mab. It was unpredictable as to whether the merchandise, useful or not, would be judged attractive or, through the same unverifiable process, be scorned and left to rot in the warehouse. The undershirts had been snatched up as had a batch of purple satin bras, but the laundry bluing was still there. It was melting in the store and every time it rained the spot grew larger, spreading all over the place and staining customers' feet.

When the stock he had been hired to sell was still on his hands and on his mind, the director embarked on desperate promotions: buy three and the fourth is free; then, buy two and get four, with little success. The inhabitants of the Model Village weren't interested. Why should they take five of those things when they didn't even want one? You had to come up with ideas, if possible divert the thing that had already deviated from its conception a hundred times, explain the thousand and one possible uses for the zipper, sell toothpaste as lipstick, syringes for enemas, toasters as fans. But the director didn't have enough imagination to deal with a populace that had even more than he had because it was used to coping. He was also honest; certainly he would never have sold those undershirts if he had known.

One of the main reasons that African Resource had difficulties was that it couldn't get hold of the village food trade. Every two days provisioning trucks would bring meat and manioc, bones and muddy flour. Formerly, when there were fewer workers, ready-made meals had been distributed to them and their families: combat rations purchased from some armies that had counted on long wars and been surprised by prompt victory or quick defeat. In them they would find a bar of quince paste, another bar of Tonimalt, two sardines in oil, some paté or rillettes, dried soup, a tablet of effervescent vitamin C, and powdered wine. There was also a dose of something to calm the stomach and a card bearing good wishes in several languages: "Bon appétit, boys!" There had never been any problem with replenishing the stock; the problems, just like always, came from elsewhere, some place you wouldn't expect: the customers, the workers of the village.

There had been a strike, and even a rebellion that was remembered as The Mess Kit Rebellion. Those idiots preferred manioc and meat, they preferred cooking for themselves, lighting the fire, wasting time, to say nothing of all the disgusting things they added – cockroaches, ants. Hello, diarrhea! The rations had everything required but they didn't want to know about that. At least, if only (and it was Ysée who said this) they had added a bit of banana to what they ate, that's so easy, but no, no banana. Bananas were revered just like gods; they didn't intend to eat any.

As for Ysée, that drove her nuts. To see this complete meal, perfectly wrapped inside its sterile peel, with the necessary glucides, lipids, "and proteins," scorned in favor of the humerus of who knows what, boiled for a long time with flour – in other words zero on the food chart. She persuaded César: at least one banana a day, a breakfast banana, a snack banana, a lunch banana, so easy to take with you, healthy, good, tasty . . . César knew this perfectly well, but the village would have none of it. OK, too bad for you, the lady hooted. If you're sick don't come complaining.

Victor asked for some paper and envelopes and the Humpback brought him the one pad of airmail stationary from the store window. Victor took the Bic meant for demonstration; he knew what he had to do now. He would write Beretti a letter asking him to revise their contract and let him leave. He wrote his grandmother also. He told her that everything was just perfect and that the reason he hadn't written sooner was that he hadn't found time, but that all the marvelous things he discovered every day made him think of her; he had thought about her every instant. The thin paper still bore indentations from the words in his letter of resignation. By daylight streaming in at a low angle the old lady would have been able to read a sort of engraving of his marks of discouragement, despair, and despondency.

Victor

Beretti didn't reply. Shipments kept on flooding in and Queen Mab kept on paying. Life was hard for Victor, harder than it had ever been; he had never expected it could be this hard. More than courage it required absolute resignation, giving up entirely. The warehouse was a trap. No matter what he did he could never get out of it; the counter marked the ultimate frontier, the one he didn't cross. He was the prisoner and, at the same time, the guard. He didn't consider fixing things up. He slept in the store on a trestle bed, washed in a sink put aside for sale, and used everything in the store the same way: a sliver of soap, a taste of toothpaste, a reflection in a mirror. He lived on what he took. When he was hungry he would take a can from the stock. He composed his menu according to the deliveries. For one month he had eaten a cream pudding whose flavor he never could determine, neither by color or taste; for two weeks it was escabeche of tuna and green beans. The dates on all the cans had well expired. The heat was so pervasive that their contents were always lukewarm and syrupy. To heat them up he only had to put them in the sun; ten minutes on the windowsill and the can's temperature was up to 150° F. It would spurt when you opened it.

In the evening he saw Guastavin sweep by in a gust of wind. Victor was now watching and waiting for this man he had sworn to avoid and he called out: Hey, Guastavin! Some kind of weather! The other man stopped in his tracks and turned partway around toward Victor, then, ready to be off again, he shouted: Big disturbance in the Irish Sea. No kidding? Victor detained him. Guastavin explained how the forward thrust of a polar air current, checked by the hot Sahara winds, was settling a mass of a stormy nature on Ireland. A "siege," Guastavin commented and wondered how they would manage. The Thames, la Tamise, he translated in reverse, had frozen. Goodbye, *a'revoir*, and off he went, kik-kik, in a hurry to see if his monkey had hightailed it. So it's winter back there, thought Victor, his heart burning with nostalgia.

One more disappointment: the teacher who had come to visit him the first week he was there. Clément was a young man, exquisitely attired and refined in his language – the perfect example of the civilizing mission of a great culture. He paid meticulous attention to himself, the way he looked, the way he spoke. He had learned several books by heart and recited entire chapters of them with the facility of a brilliant improvisation. By a remarkable bit of luck the library had belonged to the Jesuits and the books that were the source of his words were technical and scientific works dating from the eighteenth century. His language was simultaneously abstract and full of wit, also quite colorful, but in a style no one used any more. His words imprinted themselves on his body and unconsciously his movements had something both antiquated and lively about them, a great deal of reverence in his arms and thighs, a cherry red on his mouth. Clément was to the village as Bougainville was to Tahiti. The black version.

Clément expected that Victor was in his own way like a book and did not hide his disappointment in the young man who, knowing nothing, had nothing at all to say. Clément had listened to César, he had listened to Guastavin, he had even listened to

Ysée; none of them spoke at all in terms he knew, merely a few chopped up and deformed sentences, swallowed words they spit back out, nothing he recognized. It was as if language in their mouths had become crippled. Returning to the Jesuit library was the only thing that gave him any peace, opening a book to reassure himself that the language existed, though under cover. He would carefully close the book again and slip it back between the others so there would be no empty space for the spirit of beauty to escape through. What's that you're fucking with? asked the Jesuit librarian, whose language wasn't all that nice, either.

Good morning – Good evening, that was all Victor could think of to say. Clément looked at Victor's mouth from which nothing issued. Clément talked a lot. He told him about the library and the Jesuit; clearly Victor didn't understand either one. He couldn't even figure out what that meant: Jesuit library; he wasn't even sure he could put the two words back together again. That's a nice suit you have, remarked Clément, taking stock of the black derelict hung from the ceiling and swinging in the breeze like a hanged man. Victor got his voice back, he told about riding the bus with his grandmother, about Conchon-Quinette, about wool mark. Clément didn't understand, especially Conchon-Quinette and wool mark, but he was too proud to ask for clarification. The black suit, surrounded by the mystery of these strange, coarse words, seemed much less desirable to him.

Victor waited in vain for Clément to return, he felt that their youth was enough to make them get along; that's the way parents decide on who their children will have for friends: they're the same age, they can play together. It was obvious that Clément didn't want to play with Victor and Victor was mortified. He watched for the children as if they might have some message they were bringing from Clément. But nothing, and then he realized that each child was a bit of Clément; they too expressed themselves in that language he didn't understand, as if the words bogged down in a heavy accent. He watched them playing at the other end of the village; they were all around Guastavin's house.

Hey, Guastavin! Guastavin. He wanted to warn him; he had seen one of them on the roof. Had he thought about protecting the roof, too? Guastavin shrugged his shoulders. I know all about it, I've stumbled onto what's up. A woman? asked Victor, thinking about the girl. No, Guastavin replied, a man. Guastavin had long suspected it and he'd just had proof. César at the steering wheel of his jeep with the guy beside him. Victor assumed that maybe it had been one of the Banana Men and, if that were the case, they needn't worry. But Guastavin knew for sure; he had recognized the guy. His name was Gilbert. Just like myself when I had a first name, he added bitterly. He called on Victor to be his witness: this Gilbert would replace him some day. So just don't get all upset, said Victor to console him. But Guastavin didn't give a damn about any such soothing words. You know, he went on, I looked César in the face, just like that, and he saw me looking at him and he looked away. Let me tell you, he's gotten ugly, ugly; that's all there is to it. Victor didn't remember that César had ever been handsome. Yes, maybe not, Guastavin agreed, but now he's just plain ugly. Why? asked Victor, to prolong the conversation. But Guastavin didn't have time. She's waiting. By the way, how's she doing? asked Victor. Guastavin drew a triumphal, round shape in the air in front of his belly, it's growing. So, see you later: Of course, they should get together soon, but not now, not as long as she's pregnant, she can't stand people. Victor agreed. She was going through a difficult period.

At work Victor was in charge. The Humpback and the Cripple, called B and B [one B for *Bossu*, Humpback, one for *Boiteux*, Cripple], balked. They displayed the mutilations that kept them from doing any sweeping, washing, lifting, or carrying. Victor didn't dare ask just what exactly they did do. The hump that made one small body lopsided, reducing its chest so it fit a child's shirt beneath a head that was too long and had a shifty-eyed expression, and the poor leg that made the other one walk like a cricket seemed good enough reasons for them not to work at the banana plantation. But Victor couldn't stand the way they looked at him, and even more than that, their gossiping; it spread like poison through the village. They would arrive very punctually at six in the morning and at eight o'clock in the evening they took off again, banging up against each other, one worse than the next. Victor didn't know where they lived or what they lived on. At midday break they would open a package tied up in a banana leaf and squat down to eat what was inside. Sometimes Victor would give them a can that they carried off with them without opening it. It was night when they arrived; it was night when they left; the rest of the time they contemplated the day and talked interminably, a constant, endless, monotonous discourse broken by a few shrill exclamations. What could they be learning from each other that they didn't already know?

At the end of his resources and hoping for some hidden treasure, Victor opened the barrels: that they were double-wrapped, stamped flammable, and marked with a skull and crossbones were sufficient evidence that the product was dangerous. B and B came closer: Avoid contact, flammable, in case of absorption contact the nearest poison center. What is it, Boss? they asked. I don't know, Victor replied. He was hesitating between vitriol, arsenic, rat poison, and lemon-rub. Faced with this highly denatured, whitish porridge which, in the presence of air, was giving off purulent bubbles that broke the surface like thick blisters, they asked: Other than being dangerous, what's it used for, Boss? I don't know anything about it, said Victor and he thought he would have been better off leaving the barrels as they were, considering that now the warehouse stank. One of the Bs complained of having a hard time breathing, the other that he was seeing red. That's nothing, said Victor as confidently as another Beretti: That's because the chemical has gotten wet, we just have to let it dry out. They carried the barrels outside into the sunlight and, in fact, the bubbling subsided and the liquid shrank. At the end of a few weeks all there was left in the bottom of the barrels was a very fine white powder. Victor was triumphant.

Victor copied Queen Mab's technique. Watching her work in her little kitchen with her piles of a few grains, vials of a few drops, Victor thought that to make this bulk powder appealing it would have to be decanted into something tiny. He asked B and B. Great excitement. They cast about. In shoe-polish cans, Boss, said the Humpback. They spent days on end filling the little cans of Wax la Lune from which they had removed the dried-up contents. They did it carefully, painstakingly, with delicate movements, they closed the lids: a little white moon was smiling behind a saddened black moon. It was all perfectly useless but Victor was happy that he had managed to keep them busy. However, they never even finished the first barrel. Soon they were complaining of burns. One morning they discovered that the tips of their fingers were eaten away. Scarcely more than two days had passed before the skin pulled back and laid bare an oozing pulp of flesh. The chemical was even more caustic than he had thought; it seemed to have extensive effects on human skin. Far from soothing or reducing the caustic effect, water and creams seemed to increase it tenfold and the burn, because that's what it was, spread a little farther every day that went by. After their fingers it was the palms and the backs of their hands that were attacked. B and B didn't seem too worried; they'd already suffered through so much. As for Victor, he spent his time tending them, inventing compresses, ingenious solutions and concoctions. One day, although he didn't know why, the burn calmed down, at least in appearance; the open wound healed over. But B and B lost forever their color; on the ends of their black arms they had pink hands. Ordered to rest they waved their hands in front of their eyes, in light, quick figures as if what was there were wonderful butterflies or fantastic birds.

Victor still was selling nothing. In the end Queen Mab was his sole partner: he was her wholesaler, she was his banker. She took up all his time. She would spend hours turning a can of milk over in her fingers, extracting prices; but then, since she loaned him money she gave herself permission to leave without paying, all the while reminding him of his debt. To settle his accounts he was forced to agree to sell her a packet of alphabet noodles, more valuable than noodles that don't make words, and that he esteemed just as highly as the bar of soap and the can of sardines. The giantess bore it off in triumph and ten minutes later the wildly zealous and curious crowd was dividing the package among them one letter at a time. This expert stroke was Queen Mab's masterpiece in the sale of minuscule single items. What's that? she asked, seeing the round cans that B and B were using the tips of their pink fingers to put into boxes meant for melba toast. We don't know yet, they answered. We haven't decided.

As for the others, the coolies, the village dwellers, Victor still didn't know them; he glimpsed them from above and at such a distance that he couldn't see them. He watched them as in a dream, because they were dream people. He was unable to believe in their reality. True, Guastavin, true, Clément, whom he had only met once, true, Queen Mab, but not them . . . only the children at the end of the road, who were playing Fort-Chabrol. Come on now, another letter to his grandmother. And tell her what? He tried to think of something to say. When night fell all he wanted was a great silence that would close his jaws, an immobility that would paralyze him, and yet that was the time when he had to do battle against the invisible frenzy of this dark, blind, primitive life.

He hid the grain away, he locked up the flour and the noodles; there was nothing he didn't place in the center of a dish of water on fragile superstructures meant to halt the invasion of ants, cockroaches, and spiders that, fleeing the insecticide on the banana plantation, now streamed through the village. His suit was the object of stubborn desire on the part of every conceivable small creature; he had had to hang it from the ceiling to protect it from rats. The rope, the wall, the empty space still hadn't been enough. One night he had fought with a rat walking along the ceiling with its head down so it could get at the rope and chew it. The animal had put so much intelligence and effort into its operation that, when it saw it was discovered, it let out a screech of incredible violence. When Victor finally dislodged it by hitting at it with a broom, it fell to the ground with a dull thud and was instantly back on its feet to attack him. He had retreated in the face of such determination, then, crazy with rage, he returned to combat and chased the rat with a brutality that he would never have thought he was capable of, finally cornering it against a wall and, despite its cries, running it through, yes running it right through with the broom handle. A massacre.

The worst had been getting rid of the body, picking it up by the tail – it had seemed very heavy to him – and throwing it outside. Too hasty a decision, too short a throw – the rat landed close by. Victor watched for some cats to come; he trusted they would. That night none came. In the morning the body was still there. Victor couldn't take his eyes away from the stiff, dried-up shape on the sandy road. Luckily the sun came up and brought the flies. And the corpse swelled, it made little convulsive movements as if retching. It rolled onto one side, black and glistening, shook itself, took a sort of step. You could hear it spluttering. Night fell and Victor couldn't see anything anymore. But the frenetic, drunken flies banged violently against the sole lit window in the store.

The Planter's House

César's house stood in the center of a lawn. Its roof, set on pilasters, was covered with green metal. Five hundred yards away the banana plantations began: Devil to the south, Bull to the east, Banana to the north, Buffalo and Elephant to the west. They stretched on forever. When the sun was too strong the sprinklers went off and gave the banana trees a cloud of iridescent water, like rain detached from the sky, a shower of light. Lola would sit there for hours, just staring, her face concentrated on the horizon: a green line, no smell.

She was waiting for the insecticide plane to arrive; it was sputtering in the sky. It was working hard to cut deep furrows. Even though it just flew monotonously back and forth it was providing some animation above the banana plantation. It was old-fashioned and charming and seemed fragile with its hiccupping old lawnmower blades. It released the powder, which spread like the tail of a comet, something subtle and voluptuous, and also like fireworks, Bengal lights. It nosed straight up and down as frivolously as a circus toy. When it had tossed all its powder it came to take a bow by making a big loop above the house. It flew off, light and carefree, toward the city and Lola followed its silvery fuselage as far as she could, the spots of light on its wings; then she watched the cloud of insecticide slowly falling on the banana plantation. A white vapor as light as a veil. A few more minutes and the horizon emerged: straight, green, and stupid; boredom set in again.

She played with her two-sided mirror. When she held it at a distance her face seemed tiny. She had forgotten the proportions of her features; she thought she had large eyes and the mirror displayed very small ones. So I have small eyes, she thought. She turned the mirror over and the magnifier revealed an eye, a nose, a mouth – huge features, whereas she had thought they were delicate. But what seemed frightening and strange to her, even more than the shape or structure of her face, was her skin. She thought its texture, its substance, its color were hideous. She brought the mirror up close to a scar she had on her cheek; its pink line delighted her. You could see the even paler tiny stitch marks, exactly seven sutures. She wanted to scratch the skin around it to make the pink spot bigger.

When she tilted the mirror, she caught sight of a servant's gesture, a quick shadow that darted by; she caught a tiny bit of elusive sky, a fragment of the banana plantation, a refracted spectacle, giddy and mysterious, endlessly restructured in a combination of lines and abstract shapes that she never tired of and that always came back to (even though it did not contain it) the reality of César. The mutilated arm at the end of which his dried-up hand was growing stiffer, a big belly on two short, spindly legs that were incredibly agile and that he would fold one on top of the other when he sat down as easily as other people crossed their arms.

Heat, fatigue, work – he had forgotten that the girl was there. Seeing her there, almost lying down and billing and cooing into the mirror, vaguely reminded him of something, an unclear notion, like a lost obsession. He went over to her. He put his head in the mirror, a large square head suitable for a colossus. There was something imperial, or at the very least patrician about it, though weighed down by the double chin that had earned him the affectionate nickname Pighead from his friends the Banana Men. She sat up straight, caught doing something wrong. When she saw him her eyes crossed. No matter how hard she looked straight ahead they buggered off.

They were never alone at meals, there were always some Banana Men traipsing around in the vicinity and César would make them stay for lunch or dinner. They ogled her greedily. They never spoke to her and, pretending to ignore her, talked over her head to César. She heard brutal tales that upset her. About revolvers, summary executions, revolts put down. Violence hovered around them. Bananas were what they wrenched from the earth but also from the men, the coolies, whole populations that they went to get like animals they would drive from one place to another, forcing them across borders away from everything and making them acclimate to the no-man's-land of banana plantations. Because of the births and deaths they couldn't calculate within a hundred or so how many coolies they possessed. Some races were more fertile than others; they were all about equally submissive. An occasional revolt but, like the way flies get into a herd, a communicable fever. One shot, like cracking a whip, one coolie down. Gilbert didn't joke around.

She desired the Banana Men, as a group and separately, and perhaps most of all she desired the aforementioned Gilbert because he was blond, and blondness and blue eyes evoked in her a submissiveness coming from deep in her belly, a resigned and happy abandon. She desired those hairy thighs, those knotty muscles, the smells stirred up when they moved, a warm, golden odor that mingled with the aroma of roasted meat and grilled lobsters along with the fragrance of old liqueurs.

When they were ready to take their coffee on the terrace, she served them one by one; when she leaned over to fill their cups her very short dress revealed her transparent nylon panties. The air was heavy, luckily the batteries switched on and water began to fall on the banana plantation. The planters looked away and, noses in their glasses of raspberry liqueur, they talked about cultivation, profits, costs of production, recession. César stood up and with his first drunken and unsteady step did a little dance. He stretched his odd arms up over his head, joining them in a curve; he raised himself onto his toes in his leather sandals, which snapped, and, turning heavily as if executing a waltz in three-quarter time, he headed for the staircase.

They all stood and leaned on the balustrade overlooking the scene, watching him dance the death of the swan. He twirled, swayed, and then collapsed into spasms on the grass where, to the surrounding laughter, he played out the slow death throes of the swan, the convulsive movements of her dying, the final hiccup. The mutilated hand at the end of his raised arm represented the light, hollow head of a bird. All around him a pack of blacks, the congregated women and children. Everybody living under the house, between the floor, seven steps high, and the ground, all the families and other kinfolk came to watch the boss roll around on the lawn. They clapped their hands together and shouted, encouraging him to consummate his enormous orgasm. When the death of the winged creature left him facedown, his arm stretched out, palm open, streaming with sweat, panting, they applauded. César stood back up, stroked one head, slapped another; he scowled at a small child to frighten him, and the baby buried his head in the breast of a young mother, who laughed.

Finita la commedia. It was almost time to leave for Port-Banane. The Banana Men laughed heartily as they described their business down there. They slapped César on the back as a sign that they were all in this together: So, you still aren't interested? with a big wink. And since César, playing dumb for who knows what reason, just shook his head in a vigorous no; there was always somebody who answered for him: You can see he's in love. They doubled up in laughter. In front of Lola, whom they had never stopped ogling, they added: It'll blow over before we're even half started! And Gilbert, looking her up and down, with his very blue, very pale eyes and the expression that a journalist would later describe as an "icy gaze," let drop: Women! They're all floozies. And they tromped off to the brothel.

He pushed her toward the bedroom. He remembered now. They stood there facing each other. She had a wild, frantic look that was provocative. Lowering his head and gathering momentum, César charged through the doorway. He threw her on the bed and crashed down onto her. He puffed, he snuffled, he grunted. His beard tore at her skin, his saliva poured into her mouth and down her neck, his sweat made her belly, her breasts, anywhere he touched her sticky. He groped her with his hands and pried with his mouth. He chewed on her, he kneaded. Nothing. He left her naked on the rumpled bed. He was gone and she didn't know when he'd come back. Silence, peace when the door closed.

Alone on the bed, she began cautiously surveying an inch or so away from her body with the tips of her toes, the palm of her hand; she explored with her fingertips in a circle over her head; she spread her arms and legs, on display in her sleep. And then the dreams – a little heavier, a little more specific – began, so that she started to masturbate. In the midst of all the stout bodies with shapeless breasts, in the midst of all the black, hairy skinniness, in the midst of all the bloodless or purplish sexual organs dangling from gray skin, she remembered square-chested young men with the bellies of statues bearing the imprint of armor; thighs and ankles also, provided both knee and wrist were fine and strong. And more, in the center of a golden fleece (blond was not enough), a sex to awaken, a penis as white as mother-of-pearl with a rosy glans.

The Idyll

To cover up her personal weakness she wanted to seem unyielding. She followed Ysée's advice and opened the bible of feminine success the other had shared with her. The publication was twenty years old and spoke harshly to its readers, several generations of whom it had shaped up, using the Readers' Digest and 20th Century Fox as references. A certain Miss Priddy, who was responsible for the reform crusade and whose photo with its disdainful smile and haughtily arched eyebrows foreshadowed a preface filled with fulminations and disgust in which, all insidiously described as lazy so-and-so sluts, they were ordered, in the name of woman's dignity and the human respect guaranteed by America, to brush their teeth and change their underwear every day. The cost of their success, she claimed, was water, soap, and tweezers to remove stray hairs. As she read quickly through it, she was dismayed to learn that women were dirty and French women particularly disgusting. Miss Priddy, with statistics to back her, tallied up the gray straps and black nails that were enough to sicken any man (he presumably being clean)! Then came the photo of an ideal woman, a woman destined to make that same man succumb, a platinum blond with breasts like bombs. The caption certified that she not only bathed several times a day but that she groomed herself – scraping, shaving, and rubbing herself down with pumice . . .

When examined in detail the program to shape up, tone up, and beautify was quite simply diabolical, and the complexity of it gave you some idea of what a handicap it was to be a woman. Miss Priddy warned her readers: she gave them advice for last-ditch efforts, for starting from scratch with a blank page. First, there were morning exercises to develop the bust, thin the waist, flatten the stomach, slim the legs, because everybody can have legs like Marlene. Next, an angry little lecture aimed at any woman possibly tempted to quit from exhaustion. After that came the long, hard nails that had to be polished or you couldn't pretend to be a *real* woman. Finally, the essential thing: your hair: you had to hang your head over and brush it a hundred strokes like Bette Davis, curl and brilliantine it or at least plaster it flat into a smooth chignon like Grace Kelly, and cover it with a lady's hat, please!

The ideal was to be blond, a brunette never looked neat; the article didn't say this but you could guess from Miss Priddy's latent disgust that brown hair was as repugnant to her as hair under your arms. Not lucky enough to be born blond? Marilyn wasn't blond, either. To the reader's astonishment! But she hadn't fooled Miss Priddy. So then, who's keeping you from becoming blond? A bit of work and good dye, just so long as you're careful about roots, but no more careful than you have to be about pumicing your feet, polishing your nails, exfoliating dead skin, extracting whiteheads, getting rid of the hair on your legs, firming up your breasts. And you became somewhat less dubious than a Frenchwoman or a brunette!

Lola, in front of her mirror, assessed how much work lay ahead of her; not only was she not blond, she was black – still, maybe not entirely so, more brown, actually a very intense yellow-brown verging on green, and her hair, thick and prolific as Ysée had already remarked, was of a sort, in fact, even a substance that Miss Priddy had never seen in her life. Women, even Frenchwomen, didn't have that stuff on their heads. If you really thought about it, Lola's hair seemed more akin to the fur of certain animals: Afghan goats, desert sheep, Himalayan does – unless, perhaps, because of its interlacing curly loops, it belonged to the vegetable kingdom: the grasses of Abyssinia, the lianas of the Amazon, the cactus of Nevada. She was loath to touch it, dreading contact with such savagery, all those creatures, all those plants stuck to her skull, thriving on her head. She cut. She blunted a pair of scissors in it. Her hair went grudgingly, requiring a billhook, a scythe, a machete to sever the live roots and a knife to slit the animals' throats. The result was a tiny head on the end of a very long neck, the head of a shorn woman, the head of a sick child, the head of a young soldier. But that was because she wasn't blond. Blondness, especially when artificial, suppresses all vulnerability, and Miss Priddy counseled women to be inflexible, to be dreams, to be stone.

She turned to the next chapter: bleaching. Dyeing would take her around the bend on a voyage of no return. Hydrogen peroxide would do in a pinch but the cook, who didn't like her, told her that there had once been a woman here, right here, who had yellow hair; she used to put pig urine and dog poop on her hair. He could also get a pomade made of toad glands for her. She thanked him effusively. A woman who produced concoctions rubbed some fetid, green mush on her scalp and she went out in the sun with it on, even though her skin burned her.

The product had worked but less than you would think, considering the pain it inflicted; it gave her straw hair with reddish highlights, a little like those on the tail of a cow. She set out to become a platinum blond – a difficult path. Miss Priddy explained that it took Marilyn two hours every morning to become Marilyn. Lola was prepared to work three times as long; she hadn't had the good luck to be born Norma Jean. Miss Priddy recommended every sort of cleanser, every sort of disinfectant, every sort of bleach, every sort of lightener, every sort of eraser: the way Lana Turner would scour with lemon-rub, the cleanser all housewives are familiar with and keep under their sinks, and the way

Carole Lombard would add two drops of white spirit to her rinse water. "Housewives." She wrote that on purpose just to humiliate them a little more, those hairy brunettes. Carried away by her own enthusiasm, she gave all the women who didn't lock up their cupboards and consequently threatened their children's lives a piece of her mind. Which was uncalled-for; it seemed out of the question that any woman who followed Miss Priddy's program could one day have time to take care of a child as well.

Faced with the pathetic results of her bleaching, Lola felt the advice was valid; she went to the kitchen cupboard and tried to get a few drops of Clorox from the boy, who wouldn't let her have it, as well as a product called White Tornado, and another that not only bleached but disinfected and smelled like roses, reminding her of hospital corridors. In desperation she went to African Resource. Victor saw her against the light; the sun set her red hair ablaze, passed through her dress and outlined her body as precisely as when he had first seen her. She stood there, frozen in the light, waiting for Victor, who was transfixed, to ask her what she wanted. She moved her arm to pull her purse back over her shoulder and revealed an armpit that had been shaven as Miss Priddy had advised; the shadow there was enough to throw him for a loop. Then he noticed her eyebrows, black as swallows, a vestige of her former face, and he knew for sure who she was.

Her eyes lowered, she looked at Victor's feet; they were bare with fine long toes and square nails, and she could already guess just how blond he was, just how white. The girl's gaze made him feel ashamed. She wanted his feet. With the same movement that, once, had flung her in fatigue and despair onto a heat vent, she would have let herself slide to the ground, she would have laid her pretty, made-up face on Victor's feet, she would have kissed them. His desire for her, for her body seen against the light, would have flung him too onto the ground, and in a great tangle they would have calmed passions that were not the same at all, because she loved his feet and he loved her face; and when they found their genitals, singing as they were to be united, they would have moaned.

Without B and B, who were bustling around them, they would have been able to stay there in silent bedazzlement, in perfect happiness sustained at the utmost edge of a desire tearing at them to the point of tears, but with a suffering, however, that they held onto the way the acidity of certain fruits is retained, the better to taste the flavor. B and B pulled up a chair and brought a bottle of fizzy lemonade, which they opened. It was so hot that the liquid foamed in the thick, heavy glass they gave her. This is how they welcomed Ladies to African Resource. A sign of welcome, allegiance, luxury, and wealth. What would Madame like?

I'm looking for . . . , she said, glancing around the store that revealed its riches: a hundred nails in a cardboard box, a bar of Palmolive soap, a can of Kerbronec sardines, a pile of toasters. I'm looking for . . . considering the state of the store she did not want to humiliate or disturb anybody; she realized that unless she asked for a toaster she would hit on something not there, an empty spot on the shelves. Well, it's a little complicated and because it's a very old-fashioned product maybe you don't have it, which wouldn't be serious, I'd go to Port-Banane. Besides, I might not find it there, either. And when Victor heard her talking about Port-Banane, his heart fluttered as if she had said something about leaving. He, too, knew that no matter what she asked for, he wouldn't have it. He was in no hurry to hear her formulate a request that would separate them. But that didn't take into account the shrewd commercial vigilance of B and B. What would Madame like?

Dumbfounded, she looked at them closely. Her gaze alit on their hands and ran up their arms; the chemical had painted

83

evening gloves onto them, bright pink, a Schiaparellian shade – brilliant, silky, ravishing. Oh, she said, how beautiful! And B and B, studying their forearms proudly, felt the dawning of an exquisite emotion, exhilarating as well, one to which their lives had absolutely not accustomed them and which was so strong at that moment that it was intoxicating: the consciousness of their beauty. Can I touch? she asked, and they held out their arms. The skin was as soft, as satiny, as delicate, as thin as its extraordinary color implied. How marvelous! she said, covetously, in a voice full of lust. How marvelous!

It's the powder, said Victor. A list of words rushed through his mind: nitrite, pesticide, arsenic, lemon-rub . . . Lemon-rub, he said, choosing the least noxious. Lemon-rub, she said. That's exactly what I was looking for! Victory. Triumph. They'd hit the jackpot and Victor secretly blessed the fate that he had cursed. Those barrels – that's why they had come, that's what they meant: this woman whom he loved. An incomprehensible joy filled the store: Victor's joy, the joy of B and B who, for once, could provide the merchandise someone requested, Lola's joy. It's for this, she said and she touched the dry grass, the greenish straw she wore on her head, for that, she said miserably, and for this, her hand slid along her cheeks. Victor leaned over to see. On her very dark skin she had, imperceptibly, the prettiest freckles in existence, the ones that are called by the name of a butterfly.

B and B, with their keen business sense, were unpacking cartons, piling small boxes on the counter, opening them, breathing on them, scattering the powder. That's much too much, she said. Joy ebbed for the two assistants. It's an item we keep in stock, said Victor, take what you think best. Still, it's funny you should have it, she said. She wasn't leaving yet, to Victor's relief. She wasn't paying, which worried B and B. It was Lana Turner's favorite product, she told him, and he tried to remember which face had been

Lana Turner's; all he could see was Lola. She went on, No, not Lana Turner, Carole Lombard. Ah! said Victor, as if he understood better now. OK, she said, this isn't about all that; I'm being a bother. The blood ebbed back toward Victor's heart; he was suddenly very pale. Flood of hope for B and B, who were arguing over who would get to make the cash register ring.

You have something to do? he asked her; are you very busy up there? Not all that busy, she answered, she didn't want to admit that she was bored; but you, you must have a lot of work. Not all that much, he said, so as not to admit that he was desperate here. He wanted to ask her to come whenever she wanted but wouldn't that be inviting her to leave? You have to be careful, he went on, fiddling with a box of lemon-rub. She looked at him; she was a little distraught. He shook the box, The lemon-rub, you have to be careful. He gestured with his chin toward B and B's pink hands. Ah, she said, I know, it's white spirit, and she recited the advice given by Miss Priddy.

White Spirit, the new word had B and B in a dither, White Spirit . . . What do I owe you? asked Lola. Nothing, said Victor very quickly. Yes, yes, I do, she insisted, else she wouldn't come back again. So then, whatever you wish. She looked at B and B, who set an enormous price on it. Why? asked Victor. Because it's White Spirit. White Spirit is more expensive than lemon-rub. And why is that? asked Victor. Because of the name, Boss. And what does that change? It changes everything, they said. And they absolutely stuck to their guns.

White Spirit

When he looked at what the parent company sent him Victor had a few questions. He wondered: now, why powdered milk today when yesterday there was a shortage? Why sugar? Or simply, what are these pressure cookers here for? Why a truck full of food mills? Why a hundred irons? He didn't understand. Mostly he came to the conclusion that it was industrial folly. What a mess! He had heard people say it before: it's no surprise nothing goes right! What he didn't know was that, on the contrary, all these commodities arrived as the result of rational thought, to a calculated effect; the mess existed only in his mind. These products that were not good weren't bad for everybody. How could anyone here know that the pressure cookers exploded; how could they know that the carcinogenic asbestos had been taken off the market, or that the milk was irradiated . . . The merchandise did not get there by chance. The products, right from their conception and without anyone knowing about it, had been destined for the Model Village. With their hidden defects, the rust, the bare wires, the tops that had buckled, the covers with holes, the rottenness, the mildew, and plenty of other aberrations that couldn't be seen, felt, or smelled, they had been manufactured for African Resource, where Victor was supposed to dispose of them. He was at the end of the chain, the indispensable link completing the cycle of production; at the end of the world he was the drainpipe at the bottom of the sea. He remembered the game with only four coins but five players – also musical chairs where there's always one chair too few. When society overheats there are always places missing and it was precisely his place that was lacking. No surprise that they hadn't been all that picky about his references and experience back there. For the job he performed you had to be nothing, even less than he was . . . In order for the others to be able to feel like strong, clever winners he was playing the indispensable role of the idiot, the simpleton, utterly guileless, an imbecile; he was being cheated. Oh! the surprised expression on the face of the guy who doesn't get a place, subjected to laughter and jeers! He hadn't made a reservation, he'd forgotten to confirm. Constantly having to confirm you exist, you're alive, you want to live.

White spirit? B and B were the ones made happy by that stroke of genius. With their inspired salesmanship, they managed to transfer the stock into small cans with an eager speed quite unlike their usual pace. They forgot about the smell and the burn. On the contrary, they watched with satisfaction the pink patch that now stretched up to their shoulders. They begged Victor not to wait but to order more before news had spread beyond the plantation; they imagined considerable success; already they could see the great rush. Express delivery, by van. That might be another way of doing it, the powder having eaten away at its packaging. They had to give some thought to the jagged lines of corrosion where the iron was turning a strange, greenish-brownish color, the fetid odor coming from it, the white slime spreading up and down the drum; the merchandise could be described in the words you might use for a wound – nasty. B and B scraped, washed, and concealed. They "dressed the window": some cans arranged in a pyramid with a sign on top, which was not much use to the illiterate population. They wrote with chalk on a slate using the letters that their banana-teacher had taught them and tracing a few awkward characters of a word that Victor couldn't read but which, according to B and B, said "white spirit."

That was when Queen Mab appeared in the shop window – face-to-face with the cans and the slate sign. The white writing was reflected in stripes across her features and the letters elongated through the glass were like tattoos on the giant woman's face. Between the white letters Victor read other black letters, strange and terrifying. Only when Queen Mab came into the store with a man who did not seem to be from the village did the mirage vanish. Lean and bearded, the man couldn't focus his gaze and his head shook so you couldn't stand to look at him, even though he seemed handsome and rather large, in sharp contrast to the people of the village. Brother Emmanuel, Queen Mab announced.

All you had to do was watch B and B to be certain that it was a very bad sign to have Brother Emmanuel show up. They closed ranks so that the Cripple fit into the Humpback until they were united in a geometric composition setting right their infirmities – just like pieces of a puzzle that separately are ugly, too complicated, or ridiculous, but make sense when assembled – logical sense, mathematical, if they happen to throw some light on the pattern. One inside the other, leg extending hump, they attained an artistic perfection you would never have suspected when they were separate or bumping into each other with the sides that didn't fit together.

Queen Mab and Brother Emmanuel in their own way achieved a similar construction. Alone, Queen Mab seemed monstrous, indecent, all that size and weight in vain. Alone, Emmanuel, with his crazy eyes and his head spinning like a top, would have been frightening. But when they were right next to each other you understood that, together, they functioned. Queen Mab's gigantic size stood between Emmanuel and the world; any information he received came through her. Sounds, smells, colors – she translated them all for him. And, in the other direction, she was the interpreter of his archaic desires, his bizarre wishes, his hidden rages. Brother Emmanuel planted his words in Queen Mab's vast body and his menacing eye waited for them to come back out the damp earth of her mouth; he watched and waited for a word to appear; he watched it sprout and bloom and then he would pick it when it was a fragrant flower, with the private perfume appealing to his heart.

Brother Emmanuel wishes to know, she said. Victor launched headlong into confused explanations, in a rapid stutter like the frightened, timid person he was. But Emmanuel only listened to Queen Mab's music as she translated. He heard words that were light as the clouds bearing cherubs, light as the gossamer mists that accompany archangels; words luminous as the haloes of all saints, like a salty ice floe melting in the Tropic of Capricorn's sun, like burning bushes that set the mountain aglow, like a flock of doves fluttering in the sky; light, white words like the manna raining down on the heads of the faithful, like the puffs of sacred dust at the heels of the righteous, like the desert when you pray, like the shafts of light surging between tree trunks in the forest darkness, like the water that sparkles in the palms of your hands as you drink from a spring, and, for him the most marvelous thing, the smoke rising straight up at dawn from a wood fire, when women speak the first words of the first things said.

Queen Mab's mouth was beautiful as she translated the airy whiteness of the powder for him. Spirit, she said, spirit, salt, spirit, white spirit of salt, salt of the spirit, spirit of salt, she breathed on the word the way the wind puffs on the cloud it shapes, reshapes, and breaks apart and forms against the infinity of the firmament. And now that she had zeroed in on the essence of the word, she gripped it tightly between her teeth, misleading it, contorting it, tilting it in the direction of the anxious mind and grim hope of the man to whom she was giving birth the way you twist iron in the fire, the way you warp wood. *White spirit, holy spirit,* she said. And Brother Emmanuel's desire embraced the shape of the word exactly.

Brother Emmanuel wants to see, she said to Victor. Trembling, the two assistants opened the best can of their finest powder. An impalpable and very white dust spread out on the counter. Brother Emmanuel's gaze left Queen Mab's mouth and fixed upon the chemical. He put his hand out. Victor, thinking he intended to taste it, warned him but the other, not listening, left his fingerprints in the powder. Oh, ye of little faith, said Queen Mab as she closed the can and tucked it away under her veils. He will accomplish great things with the Spirit. It wasn't until after they had vanished that Victor realized that they had taken the powder without asking what it could be used for. As if they knew, as if they had waited for the chemical to make its appearance in the village, and above all for it to be *named*. What's more, they hadn't paid, but according to B and B the signs remaining on the counter were worth their weight in gold. In despair they watched the fragile trace now becoming blurry. A puff of air came in through the door and they saw the sacred characters that they had been unable to identify disappear. For a long time they stood there with their heads together trying to figure out the meaning of the vanished message.

At the drying plant rumors of Brother Emmanuel's and Queen Mab's visit made the rounds; the women passed on the details about how the spirit powder had written down the words of the *most high*. After work they went to get some idea of it for themselves. Victor had never seen so many of them; they were pitiful to see, so short, with big heads and stunted bodies, made even smaller by the dark blue loincloths they worked in. They seemed at the end of their rope, in the same state of tension and sadness he'd seen in his grandmother before, when, after working hard all day at the Favres', she still had "everything" left to do. They didn't dare go in. They went round and round the store and even dared step on the steps, but at his slightest gesture they rushed back into the street. They waited, dumb with desire – desire doubly felt because they were so tired, naked: violent desire. They desired that white powder, wanted it so badly they could cry.

Just a few weeks ago the spectacle of these women beside themselves looking at the little cans would have moved him and he would have distributed them all around. Take them and go, hide your tears. If you deny that tears are tears, or at least made of the same water as your own, (theirs are pretend tears); if, in the same way you deny hunger, suffering, and pain, (they hurt other people less than they do you), and if, making an extra effort, you transcend the hatred that someone else's pain can make you feel; if you can confront wounded flesh as impassively as you would a wounded tree, you survive. And if you manage to laugh, if you call all the unfortunate people on this earth clowns, foolhardy, imbeciles, then you win. Victor had not won yet, but he realized as he faced the frantic, blue herd that he was surviving.

He waited with the calm impatience of a fisherman who has good bait and knows the pond is full of fish. The lost time didn't matter – he would catch enough. Joy blazed and suddenly hope sprung up, strong and intact, and what was unthinkable rose as naturally as a clear, sparkling spring; yes, he would get enough, enough to leave, to pay for his return trip, enough to carry off the girl, and the desire for money joined with his desire as a lover, and his combined, merged desires came back to the desire other people had for the powder. Except it wasn't money he wanted nor did the others want just the powder. What made the "whole thing huge," as the Humpback said, was that, while pretending to desire certain things, they were hoping for others. I want Lola, Victor moaned way deep inside, enough to become cruel. And those little blue women who had cut bananas all day long, what were they so desperately, obstinately expecting?

The children were out of school now and joined the women;

they formed an independent group with their teacher in charge. Victor could sense an ardor, a violence, and a force in them that nothing could dull. They, too, wanted some powder; they wanted it so they could grow bigger, and survive, and escape the curse of the banana plantation. No, Clément told the children, no! White Spirit doesn't exist, nor salt spirit nor *esprit blanc* nor pure spirit nor holy spirit, or anyhow, they didn't exist the way they imagined; they existed only in name, a different sort of thing. So, said one of the big boys, they do exist. No, said Clément. They do exist, the boy repeated, because they have names. Clément did his utmost to explain to them that what they were talking about were chemicals that were akin but different, but that they were in no way what Brother Emmanuel had seen. It was almost nightfall – usually the time when the children swapped school language for village talk. In the street the teacher was saying some crazy, ugly, ridiculous things. For example, he was saying that the powder that Emmanuel named the spirit of purity was lemon-rub, insecticide, the stuff airplanes dropped, stuff that poisoned men. They didn't believe him; if there were two words they chose the one that was most beautiful. They had dust in their eyes.

That was when Guastavin appeared, erupting in a rage that Victor would never have thought possible. The crowd parted and in three bounds he was there in front of Victor. He gave him a shove and went into the store. B and B, who always had something bad or worse to say about him, bowed and scraped. You're selling that, he said to Victor, you're selling that, do you have any idea what they are going to do with it? Victor replied that it wasn't his problem, he had things to sell and he sold them and he showed him that there were also toasters, clothes irons. So you want to poison them! Guastavin threatened: If César knew about these dealings he would send him packing. Good-bye store, good-bye return trip, good-bye Lola. Give it to me, said Guastavin, give it all to me.

I'm not giving anything, shouted Victor, I sell it. But B and B were packing cans into cardboard boxes. Leave some, he begged, I need some! He thought of Lola, he saw their charming encounters dying away, their little conversations about nothing. A few minutes earlier he was going away with her, now all he wanted was to go on like before. Your Lola, said Guastavin as the assistants carried the cartons out, your Lola, her only thought is to get out of here, do you want me to tell you who with? With Gilbert, and Guastavin put his index finger in his mouth and made a dreadful sucking noise, wet and lapping.

Guastavin headed off toward his house. At a respectful distance all the women, all the men, and all the children followed him. Out in front B and B limped along, cardboard boxes on their heads. Victor hated Guastavin so thoroughly that he wished him dead and fiercely hoped it was the last time he would ever see him.

The Birth of the Monkey

The generator broke down. The village plunged into pitch-black dark. All the inhabitants rushed outdoors and experienced a revelation of darkness and silence that was a shock to their eyes and ears. Dawn, as the sky hesitated between blue and rose and then turned lilac, seemed to them a sign of birth. They heard a sob emerge from a malformed throat, a moan of pain that had forced its way between bone and bone, between loose membranes and stony teeth, a bellows's breath driven by lungs filled with water against a cloven tongue. The creature strained its neck, widened its mouth, ripped the scales from its eyes with its claws, and let out the cry of genesis.

The rooster didn't crow; the trucks didn't leave, the foreman didn't come out of his house; the village waited, petrified. Informed by B and B, César ordered Guastavin's door broken down. The coolies found the man's body in the entryway and in the living room, a bit farther in, the body of the monkey. Two bodies in shreds. César wouldn't even look. In the gulf of terrified silence you could hear the pure voice of the children whom Clément had gathered beneath the school awning. They were singing: "A la claire fontaine." By the clear spring.

Get that buried, said César. He rid himself of the past. For a long time he had had his sights on another foreman. Finally, Gilbert was going to be on the job. You, get a move on. He addressed Victor naturally because he was the only white in the crowd. Straighten up. Sweep. You have an hour. A corpse in that condition doesn't have to be handled any more carefully than carrion. They brought a large sheet of khaki cloth; they spread it out on the ground; they dragged the man's corpse and the monkey's, heave-ho! They flung them onto it, the man and the monkey, blood and fur, man and beast, arms and legs. Heave-ho! Coolies at the four corners picked it up and set out running at the same speed they used for carrying hands of bananas, except this time it was heavier: the dead mass bagged the cloth down in the center, the dead mass stained the cloth, blood oozed, four liters of human blood, four liters of monkey blood into a single dark streak spreading out behind them. And the voice of the children all in a line was growing louder, coming closer: "A la claire fontaine." By the pure spring.

Behind the drying plant they marked off a rectangle, one spot for two bodies. They intended to make a deep, wide hole. The shovels scraped the sand. The earth refused to open up. They forced it but had some qualms: this was a violent act, not customary. They respected the earth: corpses were to be exposed in the trees, and in the dust they cultivated the plants whose aerial roots allowed them to run lightly along the surface. At the first blows of the pickaxe the soil turned red, blood earth waiting to be paid for its suffering, eternally greedy for human bodies. Earth nourishes. Earth murders. Cycle. They had to dig down deeper between stones as white as bones and roots running through like nerves. The teacher had herded the children together around the grave where they were singing the final couplets of "A la claire fontaine," the saddest, the ones where the fellow has lost his sweetheart and it is the sorrow flowing from his eyes that is the source of the spring.

They tossed the two in a tangle into the bottom of the hole along with the earth that stuck to their wounds like plaster. A moment of silence with their hands hanging at their sides, not to pray but to catch their breath, to wait for the blood to leave their eyes. All of them, contemplative with fatigue, around the hole. And down at the bottom they saw a shiver run through the monkey's fur, a start, as if the entangled bodies gave a little jump. There was something moving, something twitching. They watched. The corpses moved. And suddenly in the midst of the dulled fur, the bloody bodies, the filthy wounds, in the red earth, two golden eyes.

The crowd shuddered and leapt back. The bravest ones picked up some rocks and clods of dirt, they brandished shovels in order to cover up, smother, bury, annihilate this living sign, this breath, this trace; they were as afraid of it as if Guastavin's soul were returning. No, shouted Brother Emmanuel, who was conducting the ceremony, no, and he threw himself into the hole onto the foreman's and the monkey's bodies. He pulled a baby monkey from its mother's fur, where it was lost and hanging on, so merged with her body that it was like a birth. A newborn baby monkey. He held it out to the crowd in his bloody hands. Queen Mab grabbed it and lifted it, held it up at arm's length, and Victor, who had been up front but had been forced back by the impatience and curiosity of the crowd, Victor, too far away, didn't understand what was happening.

At first nobody wanted to take it, and then, encouraged by curiosity, they all wanted to touch it. It was far less the circumstances of its birth than the real nature of the little monkey that made it intriguing. They wouldn't call it by name, it was a forest *one* or a mountain *one*. It was just overall frightening, made them think about spells and enchantments. It disgusted the women, who shuddered when its long hair touched them; it terrified the men because its arms wanted to hook onto them. Then they considered eating it. Queen Mab was consulted about the best way to gut and cook it. But what if the flesh wasn't edible? What if it was poison? It's the same flesh as humans, said Queen Mab: chimpanzee is white man; gorilla is black man. It would be ineffably shameful to hurt a man with a spell on him. And, as they studied the little face that was as pale as the palm of their hand, they knew how wrong they were. Suddenly the little monkey was a sickly inopportune child, very ugly and misshapen, whose existence was to be protected.

In the midst of all the confused, emotional talk the teacher raised his feeble voice. He spoke to the children: It's not human, he told them, its face is hideous, its limbs out of proportion, it inspires horror and disgust. It's a quadrumane, meaning four-handed, or capable of using the fingers that are at the ends of each of its limbs the same way man does . . . it loves bananas. Ah! said the crowd, finally discovering what something that ate bananas might look like. It is one of God's creatures, said Brother Emmanuel, and thus is worthy of our compassion. But it came from the windy region; it was wild and not a believer. Nobody wanted it.

Right away they had the idea of taking it to César. Possibly they were being mischievous; such a fertile population, where reproduction was a great point of honor, might have been taunting

César for his impotence and Madame for her sterile womb with this gift of the little monkey. They laughed and joked as they carried the unwelcome fruit to him. Guastavin's death made them brave. Done with that man, now they would surely win out over César. The crowd was getting carried away, turning into the sort of people who unthinkingly trigger revolutions. Eight hundred coolies, plus the teacher who didn't want to turn his kids loose, plus Victor, who followed along for no reason, just to be following. Eight hundred ant-men led by Queen Mab and Brother Emmanuel, in defiance of orders, usual procedures, and prohibitions, appeared at the planter's house. On the veranda, César, Lola, and Gilbert watched them coming.

Here, Queen Mab said to César, I'm bringing you the foreman's son. It's a monkey, said César. Do you mean to say this isn't one of God's creatures, like yourself? said Brother Emmanuel, stepping forward in a threatening manner. He bore death's stigmata: the earth of the grave and the blood of victims. The teacher wanted to take the children back to school but they refused. Excitement was up a notch. The eager, mirthful crowd, given real appetite by this crime, could think of nothing better than to keep right on going. It's a monkey, César calmly repeated, and, perhaps now a bit less sure: a little monkey. You say that because you are Uropean, Queen Mab retorted, and you could tell from her tone of voice that she had no use for what she called Urope and the Uropeans. Put it there, he said, pointing to an empty soap box. The disappointed crowd went away; it had counted on much more resistance on the part of the White Man. Brother Emmanuel's fists were already clenched in anger.

Lola squatted down next to the little monkey. It looked like a crumpled flower at the bottom of the box. Victor went over to her. They both pretended that it was only the monkey they were looking at. Lola explained that she had been sent out to a wet nurse who was so poor that she had made her suckle through a rag. It was just like here, the dirt hard packed and ... He went her one better. He was an old hand at poverty. Hard-packed earth strewn with fresh herbs and kneaded with straw was clean, he told her. Looking at the little monkey, she saw herself again as a nursing baby, and as Victor looked closely he pictured himself no differently. You're unhappy, little like that, motherless. People think we don't understand, but it isn't true. I can remember, she said, and beneath the halo of light in her hair her eyes glistened with tears. They stood up; the crowd dispersed, but the children were waiting.

Gilbert, described later by a journalist as having tough, strong features, "a craggy face, carved from marble," was not pleased, not pleased at all. You're not going to let those niggers push you around, are you? César replied that there was nothing to be gained from confrontation, they were edgy, you just had to let things take their normal course. But, since Gilbert was there to get things under control again, he did listen to him. First, said Gilbert, who had stuck his thumbs under the elastic of his red shorts and snapped them loudly against his hard stomach each time he said something. First, guard the house. He pointed to the spot where he would put machine guns. OK, said César. Two, get rid of the ringleaders, that mystical loony and his old bag. OK, said César. Three, teach the kids a thing or two: put them to work. We'll see, said César. And finally, pointing with his chin in the direction of Lola, Victor, and the chimpanzee: get rid of that. Of course, said César, looking at Victor and the monkey.

Victor left, carrying with him the little monkey. On his back he could feel Gilbert's scornful look but also Lola's sweet gaze. At first he walked a little bent over, red-eared, as if ashamed, but then stood up straight and knew that Lola's heart was won. He turned around and behind him, in a perfect line just as Clément had taught them, came the children, their eyes shining and a smile on their faces. Spontaneously, they broke into song: "A la claire fontaine." By the bright spring.

Back at African Resource, B and B, who had been hiding all morning long, dashed out to meet Victor. They dispersed the children. They had been to the foreman's place and dug around in everything. Not a can was left; the White Spirit had vanished in thin air. Doesn't matter, said Victor, having trouble emerging from his dream. Doesn't matter, because we have him now. And he showed them the little monkey. They refused to touch or handle it. They couldn't – not with these fingers, not with this skin. Maybe before they would have; they couldn't say about that, but now their fingers were too precious, consecrated by the White Spirit to beautiful, immaterial things, said the Humpback. Spiritual, said the Cripple.

Victor tried to write his grandmother to tell her about the foreman's death. He couldn't think what to say. He heard the monkey moving around in the soap box where he had put it on a mattress of dry leaves. It was the sound of a forest when the wind comes up. He went to look at it and took it in his arms. The little monkey made the only gesture he knew – with his long arms he snuggled up against Victor's chest and made a scarf of joy around his body, a scarf of love. Victor felt all the power of joy, as gods do at the height of libations, like a woman when she stretches out her hands and takes the child to curl up on her breast. With the monkey clasped tightly against him he went back to his letter.

The banana trees, he wrote – and as he wrote his happiness unfurled – have bloomed . . . Flowers of blood, heavy as hearts, enormous, throbbing flowers, fleshly turgescences of a purple that could only be compared to a reddish satin, violet faille, glazed chintz, with a crimson taffeta at the heart. When a petal lifts you see the deep velvety shadow of plush the color of poppies. And it all happens at once in a single night, a thousand acres, a throbbing red plain with a pungent, intoxicating fragrance.

Brother Emmanuel

When Gilbert, the fellow in the red shorts, declared the first decision of reform to be the dismissal of Brother Emmanuel, he wasn't mistaken. He had understood where the center of dissidence lay. When it came to getting rid of him, lawfully or not, it was a different matter. Touching Brother Emmanuel meant questioning the very foundations of the Model Village: its structure, its rites, its soul. Rather than saving it, as Gilbert imagined, they ran the risk of causing the permanent ruin of the banana plantation, in a cataclysmic reaction stemming not just from the history of Africa and the essence of the continent but from the world order. Meddling with Emmanuel would mean spreading doubt, disorder, and turmoil, churning up the nothingness. It meant moving irreversibly toward catastrophe.

Brother Emmanuel was the product of an abortive evangelization. This young man, now almost thirty, as a child had met a Franciscan father who, with all the despair in the world, had devoted himself to converting the most primitive populations in the most godforsaken or most inaccessible places. He went on foot, wearing sandals with soles cut out of old tires, and he performed all sorts of dangerous and forbidden acts, anything that could imperil the body, which he detested.

Father Jean splish-splashed through the mud, offering his back to leeches, his face to mosquitoes, his hands to every sort of cut and gash and slash, and his feet to innumerable stubs and bruises. He munched on strange fruits, ate raw roots and bitter barks; he drank stagnant water with myriads of insects seething on its surface. He wanted to die but before doing so he wouldn't mind going blind so he could run headlong into the trunks of trees, so he could get caught in bushes with thorns as long and sharp as needles. Because, and he blamed himself for this, his eyes let him know where there were obstacles, his feet stepped over the roots and it would have taken too much willpower to go into thorn bushes. If his eyes were blinded he felt he could relax a bit, that he wouldn't always have to be taking a rebellious body down rocky roads, the kind where your skin bleeds, where the soles of your feet burn.

He was like a shepherd tired from having to keep one particular ewe on the right path when there were herds and herds of sheep to be led to a safe place; and all because his body was alive... Then an unknown village appeared, one of those villages with an assembly house where the old men translate the world, a watering place where the children play, a wood fire kept going by the women, and a forest where the men go hunting – a village like so many others with a plot of manioc, millet drying on a mat and protected from three banty hens by a little girl. And what else? A bitch asleep in the sun with her teats swollen with milk, an adolescent who has grown a lot these past few months and has been promised he will finally be taken hunting, an adolescent sharpening arrows, polishing an old machete. Father Jean dropped to the ground.

The village people circled around him; they had never seen any whites, but their reputation had reached them through the tales of a veteran of World War II, who had been enlisted in the same division as the supporters of a soccer club that had had its hour of glory. They thought it was strange that people made so much fuss about this hairy, emaciated creature whose body was convulsed with diarrhea. They brought him some clear water and white millet; in the face of this offering he closed his eyes as if he were blind.

Then the instruction began, making use of the words at their disposal, which were not a lot. The veteran had scattered a few around, which had sprouted wherever possible. In the course of the years many had degenerated; that they might still mean what they said was uncertain. It was the lewd vocabulary of war and these gentle, happy people knew nothing about all that. Smilingly, and just to make him happy, they told the exhausted white man: Fuck off! And a small child, picking the bugs off, pulled a fat tick, bursting with blood, from the white man's neck, rolled it between his fingers, and called him – Father Jean, not the tick – "big shit!" The veteran who might have served as interpreter wasn't there.

Father Jean had seen worse. It was nowhere near enough to discourage him. For the next few months the well-meaning natives called him a Kraut and demonstrated considerable aptitude for the words of the Scriptures. Jesus, Jesus, said Father Jean. Hallie Lou, they replied in unison. Then one day the words made sense again and the Word increased in dignity. They put twice as many leaves around their waists and the women who weren't nursing wrapped themselves up to the neck in flowering vines. Catechism classes took a cheerful, languid turn, both modest and sensual. The girls all wanted veils like the one promised by Father Jean to the best behaved among them; the boys demanded puttees. The ghost of the veteran remained ever vigilant.

Baptism was necessary. They chose once and for all their first names from the list posted by Father Jean. They wanted to know the meaning of the name, if it was pretty, if it was auspicious or honorable, if the saint referred to by that name was better than another one. Father Jean taught them modesty. He refused to baptize any of them "God" or "Christ" because it just wasn't done, but in addition to the usual contingent he did authorize some Marys and Josephs. Much discussion. Barely educated, they absolutely had to debate until they arrived at the ultimate exegesis, wicked, prideful people. Why not God, why not Christ, who exist, you say, and why lots of Marys and Josephs when there was only one of each? Because God is God, Father Jean replied, father of Christ, and Mary . . . Mary is Mary, mother of Christ, they recited. And when you put it this way, they went on imperturbably, confident that sacred history and Western logic bore them out, the mother of God would be lower than God and the mother less than the son. Shut up! Father Jean commanded. You're nothing but obscene blasphemers. Shut up and pray!

Then he went back to the list. As soon as a name was chosen he crossed it out. There were some grumblers. Too bad for you! Should have come sooner. They learned dissatisfaction. The adolescent with the new arrows was inconsolable because the name he got didn't mean anything. From the start he had set his sights with all the power of his new faith: I beg you, Mary, sweet Jesus, God, Christ. He aimed at an archangel – Michael-slaying-the-dragon, a Saint-George-running-the-vile-creature-through. He wanted a holy warrior with a bow and arrows. But Emmanuel is a fine name, Father Jean consoled the desperate child, whose tears were spurting straight out through his lashes; it means the well-aimed messenger of the Lord.

Happy and reassured, the well-aimed messenger gave free rein to a joy that was just as spontaneous as his recent sorrow; his fifteen years did the rest: in his joy he raped a girl who had been granted the name of Mary. A crisis! Not because of her vanished virtue but because of seeing herself taken off the list of candidates for the blue veil. You should have thought of that sooner, scolded Father Jean, as if the girl, crushed to the ground in the wild scramble and under the weight of the well-aimed messenger, had thought about anything at all; but yes she had: pleasure. Father, father, she moaned, hoping that despite it all she might get a bit of veil, even a torn bit. Enough of that! No veil at all! But this was a lesser sorrow than the one in store for Emmanuel.

The baptisms were performed one right after the other around the backwater where, following the strict and pure tradition, a half-submerged Father Jean stood to await the catechumens. It was warm, the water delightful. They had to be kept from all diving in at once. Up in the trees white birds that looked like big flower buds were nesting. Baptized, held firmly underwater by Father Jean until they could free themselves from his grip, half drowned and all delighted, arms in the air, they cried out: Hallie Lou! But when it was Emmanuel's turn Father Jean said: Not you.

Why not me? replied God's "chosen one, his well-aimed messenger, his beloved." Along the banks joy ebbed suddenly. Not you, repeated Father Jean. He might have closed his eyes to the fornication; in a pinch he might have excused the rape. But there, in the middle of the water, what he refused to accept from the depths of his being was the life of the body, crude and violent with a puberty that was repugnant to him. This muscular chest, this deep voice, these genitals taut with life. Not you, he repeated. He became inflexible: Never. And in the roar of his wrath the white birds few away.

People were in a hurry to get this over with and someone took Emmanuel's place. Already you couldn't see him anymore. You could just hear him shouting above the hymn they sang: the Lord works miracles for me. *Why not me? Why not me?* But already Emmanuel's bellowing wasn't so loud, not so annoying, and besides how much did the one excluded count next to the happiness of them all? They had learned about exclusion. There was a banquet, a bonfire, and the awarding of the blue veil, which was a little disappointing, ordinary as the sky. Listening to Father Jean, they had imagined some color that was more rare, more exquisite. You might as well award green. Mary had just learned that the grief felt about honor is not eternal; only memories of pleasure are obsessive. She was already feeling ready for the second sacrament. After baptism marriage; it was in the catechism.

Father Jean set off on his way again. It was time. Any longer and he would have been dispensing justice under the large flamboyant tree, a few days more and they would have begged him to take a wife. They were already building a church; they wanted to set him up ... But now, his limbs rested, his wounds healed, he found his body was like a too long inactive muscle – no longer able to put up with suffering, reluctant to face pain. He had to start all over from the beginning, force it to bang into things and make it fall down. He went into the long grasses that were sharp as assegais and cut his face. That was when he began to hear *Why not me? Why not me?* like remorse, a second thought, the voice of his conscience. Because, he kept saying inside himself, because I don't love you, because I don't love you all. Then, blinded by the blood running down his face, he was pretty well forced to conclude: Because I don't love myself.

Why not me? Emmanuel was following at a distance. He saw the old man staggering. And he hurled after him all the veteran's words, warped by war, distorted by the supporters of the soccer team, forbidden words, words of despair over a bungled goal, a dubious referee: Motherfucker! double-crosser! fag! Father Jean observed that anger got the words straight better than love did and that Emmanuel was certainly saying what he meant. He might still have calmed him down, baptized him, given him peace with a little mud and a bit of bark. He didn't turn around. Then chunks of wood began to hit him in the back, fistfuls of dirt, rocks. He could tell he had about had it this time and an infinite joy came over him. He still might have baptized Emmanuel with a bit of blood and saliva, but this was too beautiful an end.

Emmanuel leapt onto him, threw him to the ground, and

gripped his neck. Crouching over him, bashing his head with a big rock, spittle at the corners of his mouth, right next to his face, Emmanuel asked, *Why? Why?* And Father Jean, who a few minutes earlier had obeyed a powerful instinct composed of disgust and unlove, saw things as they truly were, as only the death that is not at all surprising can reveal them. He choked out the words of love: Emmanuel, Well-aimed Messenger, Beloved of God, I love you.

In the monk's knapsack there was a packet of chicken noodle soup that one of his benefactresses had sent him last Christmas, and in a cough-drop box he had a few hosts, a small, gloomy crucifix, and a Bible that he was weak enough to be attached to because it had belonged to his mother. Emmanuel helped himself to the soup packet, the cough-drop box, the little crucifix, and the old Bible that had lost its gilt, and walked straight ahead. His beard grew. One day he came to the Model Village; that was a very long time ago.

He dropped to the ground near the well on the outskirts of the village, all his strength gone. Along came a woman; she was very tall, very beautiful, and above all, big and solid. She threw a bucket in and pulled up some water. Then she noticed him. He drew back, afraid. She took a tin cup and poured him some water. He drank. She began to wash him, his head, his shoulders, his face. She cleaned the dirt from his feet with her bare hands, scrubbing and caressing at the same time. My name is Emmanuel, he said. I'm Queen Mab, she said. With her teeth she pulled a thorn from his heel. And then she helped him up; he couldn't stand. She wasn't huge yet but already she was strong, sturdy enough to support him; she picked him up and carried him in her arms. He lay his head on her shoulder and closed his eyes. When they came into the village it was dusk; the men had finished their day's work. She told them: This is Emmanuel, the Messenger of the Lord, he's coming to give us the word; he's coming to name you.

The Monkey's Baptism

Brother Emmanuel preached a religion combining something of Father Jean and also something of the war veteran who had learned about life from the outrageously crude supporters of the soccer team. He worked wonders and turned out to be an effective and dedicated Baptist. In no time at all he had their passivity organized and began to baptize the village, baptizing and baptizing – so many that he had to do it by threes. Triplets in God, they were bound together by a single name. George belonged to three strapping fellows, banana plantation coolies who were so alike that you might have thought friendship had blown the same name their way. Theresa, on the contrary, was shared by a respected elderly woman of forty-five, a puny girl of fifteen, and a fat one who was twenty. The latter, one suspected, once the other unnecessary shoots were pruned away, would carry off the distinction of occupying the entire name on her own. The schoolmaster was not in favor. He thought that instruction had to be dealt with on a personal level; he didn't like calling on Michel and seeing three pupils stand up. He amended their names: Michel-the-good, Michel-the-small, Michel-the-squinter. That's how dynasties are founded.

Once he had cleared up the backlog Brother Emmanuel confronted present reality. He was passionately absorbed in the daily baptisms, the births that were the despair of the Fine Ladies and the joy of the inhabitants of the Model Village. At the first cry he rushed right over and said: What shall we name him? The happy parents replied as one: Whatever you think, Brother Emmanuel. There was nothing he liked better than naming. Running a bit low on Christian names, for a while now he had been taking his inspiration from the soccer team and from whatever was written on the canned goods. Gloria Milk. Does Gloria suit? Hallie Lou! the happy parents replied. All had to be named because life is the name. For difficult births he had prepared a baptismal syringe, half enema and half douche, that Queen Mab wielded authoritatively in emergencies.

Queen Mab – what would he have been without her? This gigantic woman was the reality of his dream. She, of all the people in the world, was the only one to have recognized him and she put everything she had into establishing him among them. She was his mother and his father, she was his priest and his apostle, she was his voice and his music, she was his speech and his writing, and when some ordeal gave him a fierce pain in the neck or hammered him in the forehead, when his throat clogged up with anger and tied him hand and foot, when his penis went erect – sadness was dreadfully arousing for him – she would hold him to her belly and he came back to life. Queen Mab had become, incestuously, his dear sister; he was her dear brother Emmanuel. It was his ambition to form a Priest-couple with her, a Pope-couple, a God-couple, because, as she said, God created it man and woman . . . and they were man and woman, the complement to that it.

She was an effective assistant not only for decorating the altar or for the choir, with her beautiful voice, but because she knew everything he didn't know and especially because she felt the music of words. She put on the glasses that could read; she opened the book. He was filled with enthusiasm; things that were mere truth entered his heart as if written just for him. At services he would recount what he remembered like a vision that had come to him. He said, with the music of words: I see. And the faithful, hanging on his every word, heard things his own lips didn't know how to say. He saw the sea, the ocean, the streams and rivers risen up as one into the heavens, and the people sitting there before him going under the monster wave. I see an ark carried along in the storm . . . I see a blazing mountain . . . I see a wonderful garden where tears no longer fall, the belly no longer groans, the head no longer suffers, the hands no longer tremble . . . He assured them that they were all in his dreams, he saw everybody, he lost no one, and because of that they had the strength to carry on. His dreams were their entire portion of happiness in this world.

Between the two of them they also performed miracles and cured the sick. Their methods were harsh. An informed witness could have seen that Father Jean's influence in these matters had been completely overwhelmed by that of the war veteran. Things grew just as heated for a sick person as for any enemy; the ears of the invalid got a good washing, with all the "filthy krauts" backed by the team supporters' vilest belching. As anger reached its peak Brother Emmanuel would begin striking the patient, pummel-ing him with his fist, kicking at him with his feet and would have enacted the murder of Father Jean in ritual if Queen Mab, in her magnanimity, had not intervened. She assured the patient, now sobbing in terror and pain, that he was healed. They had healed the Cripple and the Humpback from the Resource in this man-ner. Whenever these two saw so much as the tip of Queen Mab's turban they began sweating – which explains the fear they felt when they saw Brother Emmanuel come through the door to the store once again.

It cost him a lot to do it. Ever since Father Jean he didn't like being around whites; it pained him just to look at a specimen of this race that had wanted to exclude him for all eternity. However, in the end, there was someone to be given a name in the store. But for the fellow's tone of voice and his assistants' terror, Victor would have laughed it off, but it didn't take long for him to real-ize that if he refused he might as well lock himself in behind barbed wire like the foreman. He said he would think about it.

Don't think too long, Brother Emmanuel replied, because it's not good for creatures not to have a name.

It's a monkey, Victor tried to retort.

Lord! said Brother Emmanuel, beseeching the heavens – it was just like having to go back to Genesis for this white and therefore narrow-minded man. One day, he began, a very long time ago . . . the Humpback and the Cripple had moved closer . . . two young men of the village had lost their way in the tree forest and, dying of hunger, they fervently begged God to help them. Their wishes were fulfilled because a plate filled with succulent dishes appeared before them. The Humpback and the Cripple, along with some others, the faithful of the faithful who had dared come into the store, were so impressed they rolled their eyes . . . The young people therefore had a great feast . . . The audience in a fever of excitement. But when they were full, "the two birdbrains" took it into their heads to make a certain use of the container that had held the miraculous food . . . and here Emmanuel's voice broke with sorrow . . . using it to, using it for . . . And so God, merciless, turned them into monkeys . . . And, as resolute as God, he looked at the crowd.

That's not in the Bible, said Victor.

And a monkey, have you seen any trace of a monkey in the Bible? Victor didn't know. Did you see a monkey in paradise? Did you see one in the Ark? So, just what is a Monkey? The Monkey doesn't exist, because Monkeys are the race of Babel . . . And with these final words he turned on his heels. The assistants, standing around the box containing the one without a name, trembled: Name him, Boss, name him, name him! and their eyes were wild.

Apparently Brother Emmanuel had really gotten them worked up. Everyone at the Resource fought to give the best example of the humanity and immortality of monkeys – a wandering human species that had been struck dumb, that not only did "everything" like men, but also knew how to make war. Monkeys had been seen in troops three or four thousand strong, maybe even more, fighting with spears and arrows. People knew of a country governed by monkeys with a president-general who wore such a brilliant uniform, with so many decorations, that even the most bedecked of dictators would have paled beside him . . . And apparently Guastavin's monkey did everything the same as a woman. Because you saw that with your own eyes, you know, said the Humpback. They drink from glasses, eat from plates, and even use toothpicks!

At this juncture Lola arrived. Victor had not seen her for months, in any case, not since he had carried off the little monkey. The little monkey? She had forgotten. She wanted to show Victor the miracles worked by a hairdresser in Mégalo and pulled off the chiffon scarf keeping her hair in place: tight little curls like little snails. Do you like it? she asked. He smiled at her. That's going to take some maintenance, he said, a little jealously. Yes, she would go every week. In that case, he thought, he would have preferred she'd kept her singed and frizzy hair.

He told her what was going on. She leapt at the occasion, delighted. As a little girl she had playacted masses and marriages and baptisms with the little boy next door, who was extremely disturbed and performed strenuous Elevations and Contritions to disguise a consuming desire; dressed as a priest and frustrated enough to scream, he watched the little boys and girls he was marrying seal their vows of union with voluptuous kisses. Yes, they'd baptize the monkey; yes, it would be fun. She wrapped the nameless one in her white scarf. The Humpback went in search of Brother Emmanuel, the Cripple rounded up the population.

While they were waiting Lola said to Victor: I'll be the godmother and you'll be the godfather. But the name? he asked, we need a name. No need to worry, she was very good at names, it was a habit she had picked up being alone so much: she populated her world by naming everything. She was, without realizing it, putting the finishing touches on Brother Emmanuel's work. She had named her powder Anna, and the airplane that flew over the banana plantation Félicien, and her armchair Absalom. She bent over the monkey and looked very intently, very deeply at it as if to divine the essence, the mystery of its nature. You'll be named Alexis, she said.

And what shall we name him? asked Brother Emmanuel.

Alexis, they replied.

And what does that mean? Brother Emmanuel asked.

The one who doesn't speak, replied Queen Mab. Victor and Lola agreed. They were very happy that the name had a meaning and that it was a meaning reminiscent of animality.

Brother Emmanuel approved: This name is suitable and good for one of Babel's offspring. Alexis, he said, Alexis, son of Babel . . . and at that point his speech raced out of control, words he didn't know and that frightened him spurted from between his lips. Inside his mouth his tongue grew as tough and long as the tongue of a snake. It was all he could do not to let it fly out between his grinding teeth. With its golden eyes the monkey followed the movements over its head, the flame they were waving and the creatures moving closer, their long noses as flexible as a trunk, and then smooth, pressed skins, soft, silky, smooth cheeks. On the tips of the fingers of the female holding him there was red; there was the smell of light and the music of shouting children that moved in streams of joy, Hallie Lou, the infinite purity of a choir. It didn't have a beginning, it didn't have an end and yet, something had happened.

The Lesson

What's this? said Clément to the children when he learned that they had served as altar boys, sacristans, and choir in that farce. Can't you see with your eyes, think scientifically? That animal, whose face you have looked at closely, is the ugliest and most disgusting of all the mammals; it has a big fat head, a broad, flat face with no hair other than eyebrows; its face is covered with deep wrinkles of white skin; it has a too small nose, a very big mouth, very thin lips, teeth that are big and too yellow, and hands that are hairless, whereas the rest of its body is covered with long, black hair . . .

The children weren't convinced. That was not what they'd seen, or else what they'd seen was not a monkey. But they were used to having what their teacher said never correspond to reality. A few felt guilty about this; they would have liked for their vision of the world to be modeled on the teacher's and they made what Clément called "laudable efforts." The others couldn't care less; one part of the day they saw and heard certain things that they would express in a particular language; during the other part they saw and heard other things that were said differently. They were pupils who did not "apply themselves." The trouble with the monkey was that he was part of a world to which the teacher had no access and yet he strove to translate this world into scholarly language.

Monkeys, Clément went on, unable to stand the fact that he was not convincing them, left to themselves, live on fruits and roots in the woods; they sometimes live in trees, where they often build themselves little huts out of intertwined branches so they can have shelter from the assaults of weather; they are robust, agile, and bold, they keep each other company, use sticks to defend themselves, are not afraid of elephants and chase them off their property . . .

So they're like men? asked one of the children. He meant: so they're happier than men? The teacher saw the danger. Considering the proximity of the animal world, it was tempting to see a single nature, the equality of species. But if there was one thing the teacher was persuaded of, it was that man was superior to the other species. The monkey, he told them, is a preliminary sketch for man. It seems that *nature* (he sounded out the word so that there would be no confusion in their minds) had taken pleasure in making multiple images of man. But the monkey is only a caricature of man, or rather, a condensed version of his flaws and vices, as if *nature* (he emphasized the word that replaced God in what he was saying) had taken mischievous pleasure in showing men what they would be without *reason*. He carefully articulated the word.

In general, monkeys are unruly; their movements are abrupt and their mobile faces grimace a thousand different ways – playing the fool, we call it. Combine this with their ridiculous, crazy antics and we call it monkeyshines – a spectacle of pantomime that couldn't be funnier or more amusing. But they are inclined to steal and tear things up and break things. They delight in being dirty; they almost always have runny noses and like to suck the mucus into their mouths. They're considered shameless creatures and you have to avoid showing them to women and children up close, especially at certain seasons; because then they apparently think it great fun to display the most disgusting lubricity. In addition to other filthy expressions of reckless passion, they grind their teeth, which looks more like a sign of rage than love. Women are very afraid of them because when they find women in out-of-the-way places monkeys jump on them . . . Clément could tell from a certain quality to their silence that he had captivated the children with his talk of grimaces and antics; he had enchanted them by revealing the monkeys' flaws and fascinated them when he began on the vices with sexual connotations. I stop right here. Danger.

He paused for a moment and looked at the children to gauge their reaction. Good, he said, I see that you have understood and will not fall into any of the foolish superstitions held by ignorant peoples. Draw a monkey. You can take it back to your families tonight and restore the truth according to nature, reason, and science. The children were extremely enthusiastic, the way they always were when told they could draw. First Clément handed out pieces of paper. Each child had to make do with a quarter of it. It's going to be a little bitty monkey, said one of them sadly. Clément explained that, if you respected the proportions, you could make a small square hold a big monkey . . . They were in such a hurry to get started that they went along with this explanation though they weren't really convinced. Then Clément proceeded to distribute the colored pencils, which he kept locked up. Most of the children demonstrated some sense of realism by choosing brown, black, and gray, though they regretted that, when finally they could use the pencils, it had to be such sad colors. Michel-the-small wanted blue, red, purple, and yellow. No, said Clément, you don't need those to color a monkey. It's not for the monkey; it's for around it. You still don't need those, green is plenty. And Michel-the-small, who was a great painter at heart, was extremely put out.

They worked with relentless zeal, nobody budged or made a sound. Sometimes they would ask Clément to sharpen their pencils. A job he reserved for himself, first because he wanted the sharpening done without wasting pencil and then because the blade of a pencil sharpener in their hands could become a thing to be feared. He walked up and down the rows, glanced at their work and, following the rules of pedagogy, forced himself not to intervene, even when he saw hands go completely off-track, even when he realized that Michel-the-painter was going to draw all the leaves of a gigantic tree before he even got to the monkey, a sort of painterly digression. Luckily some of them, even the majority, were scribbling in the fur, hair by hair.

Finished, said Clément, we'll put down our crayons. George-the-big collected them. Before glancing over the drawings, Clément examined all the pencil leads, now a good deal shorter. I'll have to cut back on drawings of the earth or the forest or animals. Next week they'd draw something marigold pink and tangerine orange; he was sure to find something in a book. Show me, he said. They held up their quarter sheets of paper so he could see. Like that, at a distance, they looked fine. But close up it was a catastrophe. All the children had graced their monkeys with human faces stretched out into a broad smile. One of them had even put lace-up shoes on him, a very rare thing here but he had once seen them on the feet of a white man, an agronomist, the one who had recommended the insecticide that makes you drunk. Another child had dressed the monkey in red shorts like the ones worn by the man called Gilbert. As for Michel-the-painter, all he had drawn was a tree. And the monkey? Clément asked despondently. He's inside, replied the child. That was too much for Clément. He gave the boy a zero.

Snow White

Each time Lola paid a visit to African Resource she was slightly more blond. The young woman's soft, amber skin had become chalk-white and, almost like a moon, accentuated the full curve of her black eyebrows. She noticed how Victor looked admiringly at her eyebrows, which reminded him of the face she used to have, and interpreted his gaze as a reproach.

A few days later all that remained of them was a thin plucked arch, bleached and drawn back in with a pencil; it would have been fashionable years ago. He could have screamed. She felt his disappointment and thought she might have to go even further, maybe pluck her lashes. To hide her embarrassment, she pretended to be cheery and impetuous, putting on an air of dreadful frivolity that was belied by her unforgettable voice: a wounded, or rather a wrecked voice, the voice of a very, very little girl, no proper accents (no *aigus*, no *graves*), just a plaintive lisp limited to the range of a moan, with the choppy inflections of breathing obstructed by sobs. Hearing her was like hearing a child exhausted by grief. You wanted to open the door.

Luckily, she didn't talk much. Self-presentation required so much else that she rarely had time to talk. Besides, she had nothing to say. Being with the monkey, however, triggered something. She took him in her arms, she wrapped him in her white scarf. He would stick out a hard, knobby index finger and, with his amethyst-colored nail, he would gently play with a pearl button, just twisting it a bit. Sometimes he would fall asleep on his godmother's lap.

After the first days spent in a soap box, which, no matter how you looked at it, was not a very good beginning, she, too, had had a godmother, who was in fact a sort of aunt but paid by Social Services to take her in and be her nurse. The family got money from public assistance – so it wasn't really love but they pretended and made up little stories. The certified nurse became a godmother, like a good fairy godmother; then the child pretended she was a queen and the godmother joined in the game and called Lola "my princess." A fairy tale, you see!

But really, she was a little girl like all the others. She was messy and put on airs, which irritated these country people who were great sticklers about the cleanliness of their bathroom and the neatness of their mail-order living room, but not all that kindhearted. At twelve Lola was still the princess, but, as her godmother said: Princess Caca. Which Lola demonstrated soon enough. Her godmother, going through a difficult change of life, had taken money sent by the state – all that Lola might have spent in a year on love comics, colored pencils, and candy, scoubidous and pink plastic barrettes – and had given her a white wool bathrobe lined in fake satin, like a movie star's. The first morning, first breakfast, the cup of chocolate spilled. Filthy! but stylish! The words stuck as firmly as the chocolate puke that wouldn't come off the front of the garment she then wore every morning, unarguable evidence right up to the very last day, the day that Social Services had ceased to pay and she had slammed the door behind her. She left them the bathrobe, spot and all, but could still hear the witch's shouts of rage in the doorway. Fine, Snow White! Nice!

All that humiliation rose back up inside her. She gently rocked the monkey and he hugged her tightly in his arms; she was his mother, she was a branch, she was a tree, she was a nest made of branches where the tree limbs forked, a nice cool nest filled with green grass. She rocked the monkey and wondered how she would ever wash off so much shame.

Do you sometimes get white shoe polish? she asked. He had nothing but always stood up to go see what there was on the empty shelves. At that particular moment he had lampshades. She asked for laundry soap, whichever one washes whitest; she asked for Clorox. Laundry soap, she couldn't manage without it. La Croix, Ajax, Phénix, resurrecting names. She was all explanations and excuses. You know, she told him, I can't stand dirt; I hate stains and white things are never white enough. You know, people think that white soils easily, but that's wrong because the least little spot shows when things are white. You can wash them right away. The monkey, awakened by all this talk, opened his eyes; above him he saw the mouth opening and closing. A large branch full of red fruit that you can pick, a branch you can put in your mouth and eat; lips know how to find the sweetness at the flowers' heart. He pulled himself up to the talking mouth and licked it. It was just the way he liked it and he began to suckle. The mouth had more flavor and sweetness than he expected but was less juicy, less pulpy, maybe a little stale. Speechless. It was unspeakable but it was good. He's going to get you dirty, said Victor, taking the monkey from her. At the word dirty her mania was off and running once again.

Besides, even when there aren't stains you can see the dirt, it's dingy. I can't wear a dress or a blouse two days in a row because it gets faded here, and she pointed at her collar, her low neckline, she spread her arms to show a potential ring and then she stood up and, turning her back, demonstrated where it gets rumpled under your butt when you sit down. I hate cotton, it shows. And it showed her in all the desirable spots, her pubis, her bottom, her breasts. As for Victor, he was mad with desire. You just don't know, she said, how much I bathe. I could spend days in the bathroom; she liked exfoliants that erase wrinkles, cleansing masks that go way down deep, she wanted products that worked her skin all the way into the heart of the cells, so she could be deeply clean; she sang the praises of antiperspirants that dry you up at the source. And Victor, who felt the crown of dampness on his forehead, his underarms becoming saturated with perspiration, sweat leaving a stiff patch on his back between his shoulder blades and also running in an inexhaustible stream down to his navel, this man who was wearing his black wool suit, who never had any soap to sell and only owned one small cake of soap whose surface he caressed so as not to use it up, felt miserable. It was as if she had been taken away from him a second time.

And Lola, who felt despite all this that something wasn't quite right, who had offered him her body using whiteness as an intermediary, who had named for every product a place on it, suddenly withdrew the offer. It doesn't matter, she said. I'll go to Port-Banane. Hearing that, he felt madly jealous. Port-Banane meant Sunset and men. You're right, he conceded. I can't have everything here. He had nothing. He pretended to be above it all, someone who doesn't have time to spend on such useless things. Excuse me, she said to him. It was starting all over again, the moment she believed in somebody they would ditch her. She had come to give herself, to tell him that, if he wanted, she preferred him to everyone – César, of course, but Gilbert, too. She had put on her whitest clothes, she had waited for her skin to become truly white and her hair to be blond. She had assured him of her cleanliness, she had demonstrated that she was like an American woman, or almost, and this was the result. Dark. Gloomy. Unfriendly. Jealous. She was glad she hadn't broken with César or Ysée – who took so much persuading. Where would she be then? Out on the streets.

The Garden Party

No public announcement of the day of the garden party at the plantation. Ysée didn't want to serve her girls up to society, just toss them out into the sun with no makeup or sound system. Woman is a mystery; the day she loses that she is no longer a woman. No Visitors. César sent the Devil's Banana trucks to the Sunset. They brought the girls – light dresses, big straw hats, flower garlands around their necks. They were coming for a breath of fresh air, to get back on their feet, said their boss.

They set off in an enormous convoy of bundles and good humor, the drivers and their assistants putting far more enthusiasm into the accomplishment of this mission than they ordinarily did for a mere load of bananas. They knew where the girls came from, and, even though they'd never seen them at work they had a good idea of the practices in which they indulged. Consequently, as they helped the girls down from the high truck cabs, they fingered them gallantly, desiring a good deep feel of this elastic flesh whose price they could not afford and which was the subject of so much discussion. The girls protected themselves as best they could; they covered their bare necks and shoulders with their hands and presented what was below to the concupiscence of two or three attentive, rapturous gazes. They spread their hands flat over their skirts and abandoned their curvaceous bosoms defenseless to the incredibly precise groping of the temporary helpers suddenly popping up out of the ground to spare them the dangers of jumping. What are you doing, girls? Ysée asked. It seemed to her that the unloading process was taking too long. We're coming, Madame, they replied, abandoning at all costs their shoulders, knees, and elbows. We're coming . . .

They had brought vast quantities of grub, as if they were going to have to stay for a week. Ysée, after she'd overseen the unloading of the girls, supervised the transfer of their food. She shouted out the menu to the boys carrying the bundles: Careful of the foie gras, careful of the eels, careful of the creamed herring! She rushed to the kitchen, questioned the cook. She opened the cupboards and the freezer, picked up the pots and pans, stuck her index finger into sauces; with one sweep of her hand she straightened the cook's collar, tied the kitchen boy's apron – and dashed right straight on to the bakery. She shouted: Girls, girls! Bread, come see the bread! And when the girls showed up like hens called to their corn, she had already fallen victim to a new discovery somewhere else, with the result that the ones who got there last had no idea what they were supposed to be admiring. Luckily, another shout from Ysée put them at the front lines of some other more or less unexpected domestic spectacle.

Back onto the terrace in a great surge. Ah! ah! cried Ysée, the country, how much I love the country! And for the group's edification: That's the reason it was just no good in Hollywood, I'm a woman of the earth. The country! The girls squinted at the banana plantations in the distance and went into ecstasies, how beautiful the country is . . . and it really was very beautiful with all the water pumps pumping. I want to pick some bananas, simpered one of the girls; me too, cried the others. Well then, go pick some bananas, Lola will show you how. Lola's heart leapt in her breast, beating hard with great thumps. So she hadn't forgotten her, she had even remembered her name; Lola's heart beat with gratitude. And she led them off to the banana plantation. After they'd gone about six hundred yards over the bristly grass that, from a distance, had looked like lawn, they were sorry they'd ever thought of it; just another quarter mile, said Lola, who had never been this far. The girls were already very red. Especially considering, said Pretty-Blue, that I don't like bananas; me neither, said someone else. But Ysée had her eye on them, watching from the terrace, so they definitely had to go all the way and bring something back.

You see, César, Ysée said as she went up to him and took his arm, sometimes I think to myself – her face wore the serene air of contentment of a mother satisfied with her offspring – what is more beautiful than young girls frolicking in a park? For a long time César ruminated in silence over the phrase: Frolicking? What does that mean, Ysée? That, she replied, pointing at the girls returning, out of breath and exhausted, to the house. That, just that.

Like well-brought-up little girls who have curtseyed properly and then escaped the approving glances of their family, the whores were saying dreadful things. Goat poop, old lady! When they saw that they were scandalizing Lola they laid it on even thicker – minor obscenities, permissible bad language, it felt like the reformatory: drat, blast, puke (which was the last word in elegance) but not shit, never. They waved wildly toward the house: Yoohoo, yoo-hoo, old lady! They came closer and Ysée, who was leaning over the balustrade, wanted to know what it was they were shouting like that, and they cooed in their little-girl voices: Just having lots of fun, M'dame Ysée.

They sat down at the table. Ysée served them their portions and supervised their manners. Love-Amour, your elbow; Sweet-Bonbon, you've dropped your fork twice. Ysée made a V of two fingers and shook them at her as if she were drying a salad. This is so nice! said one of the girls. Well, now, César, did you hear what Pretty-Blue said: It's so nice! Pretty-Blue said it again: It's so nice – delighted, the way one is, in a particularly felicitous expression. It's so nice, crooned Pretty-Blue, who had found the right key. What's the matter with you, Pretty-Blue, in the end that's pretty annoying. You'd think it wasn't nice back home.

Lola looked at the whores as enviously as a neglected child watching spoiled children who are so dreadfully used to happiness. They seemed perfect to her; they possessed the ease one only gets from having been loved, when you can make up things to do and words to say without having them turn back on you, as violent as a slap in the face, taking your breath away with shame, leaving you to cry all night because you said them and full of self-hatred.

They moved out onto the terrace. Ysée unconsciously repeated: How beautiful it is. How beautiful it is, said the girls; which it was, but, the sprinklers now having stopped, much less than they proclaimed. The heat demanded a nap and the food required belts be loosened and yet this was the moment that Ysée chose to start them up again; her hustle and bustle was as overwhelming as the sun. When they sat down she made them stand up: You can't just hang around doing nothing! When they moved she ordered them to sit down: Can't you hold still for a minute? Never satisfied, always on the move. This was a person who would assemble an entire floor full of whores to find out *who* had stopped up the brothel toilets. In the most intimate hours of darkness: calculations, revelations, denunciations, punishments; they sponged it up and forgot until the next time.

But they were loved. Of that Lola was sure. They were loved by Madame Ysée, who wasn't even looking at her, even though she had done everything she could with what was available. Comparing herself with real professionals, she knew it was makeshift. Her timidity down the drain, she mumbled, So classy! What an outfit! to one of the girls, as obsequiously as poor people who think they have to like and admire everything and assure the universe of their eternal allegiance: How beautiful it is; she dared touch the fabric and turned it over in her fingers. Silk, it's silk because people "notice silk," the girl recited automatically. It's cotton, Ysée interjected. Her ears pricked and cruelty at the ready, Swiss cotton because, dearie, let me tell you, elegance is knowing how to adapt one's clothes to the circumstances; the girls would have been ridiculous with their evening gowns, and I can tell you, they have some very beautiful ones . . . And Lola, who was dressed to the nines, felt as naked as if her lamé dress and chiffon shawl had fallen to her feet. Ysée finished her off: And let me tell you, when you want to make yourself beautiful the first thing to do is wash. Dirty and a flirt, the curse was back. For a moment she thought she heard her godmother's voice and it made her strong enough to cry out.

But I'm white! she protested. She held her arms out to make

Ysée aware of the fact; there were still some traces of a white plaster that she hadn't quite rinsed off. And I'm blond, she said, calm now, a bit astonished that she had flown off the handle, made a fuss, and she scrunched her hair around. You could see the roots, like black string. Yes, so you are, whispered Ysée in reply, but you're doing it the wrong way, you're going to wreck your skin if you keep on like that, you're going to wear it down so much that it will crack, and when you have canker sores, abscesses, and ulcers you'll be just as disfigured as a leper. Lola's arms trembled. Come to the Sunset, the hairdresser will fix you up and the beautician will give you what you need. She was going to the brothel! It was still only to save her skin but she would get her foot inside. César agreed on her behalf and then, because it was time for a siesta, he closed his eyes, opened his mouth, and snored.

At the Sign of the Angel

The letter from his grandmother took two months to reach him. On the envelope, in artistic letters, she had written a magnificent address in which she had provided all his titles and a few others as well because she liked them. As a result the letter had gone right to the top, it wandered off to the Management Office, Papa's, in Port-Banane. Along the way it awakened the memory of certain debts that Beretti recalled in large letters across the envelope: "And repayment of the loan principal?" scrawled heavily in red pencil on top of all the Head Directors and other glorious epithets. Victor was extremely annoyed with her.

The letter was infinitely indulgent, the way his grandmother always was. You did well, was the only thing she knew how to say, the only thing she was capable of saying, loving and approving as she was. Seeing in black and white that he had done well depressed him enormously. He had done well to stand up against his teacher and the rural policeman; he had done well when he got angry with his friends; he had done equally well when he made up with them. He did well when he did nothing; he did well when he did something wrong. He didn't know what it was to do well. You did well, she told him, and Alexis is a very pretty name that they, the Misses Favre, liked very much.

What had he written that had played such havoc with her imagination? Or was the reality of his life quite simply so extraordinary that all she could see reflected was its violent, marvelous magic? For her, he was a father now – father of Alexis. It had been publicly proclaimed, confirmed by the Misses Favre, repeated with every pound of split peas or white beans she had weighed out that morning. With every box of detergent she had said, I'm the great-grandmother now of baby Alexis. It was her day for celebration. Queen for a day. How did she answer the more specific questions, the ones that were curious or spiteful? He could see her smile, such a good face, screening her from anything bad. She had written this letter as soon as she could, you've done well, you are my comfort, you are my life and I love you so much, you know, that I'm glad you're not here, my happiness would be too strong, it would wear you out . . .

Then a package came. Brown paper and frayed string. You could tell by the knots that old man Favre had had a hand in it; ever since he'd gone senile he wrapped all the village packages. His sisters would whisper: if you have a package to be wrapped bring it to him; he does such a good job and you'll make him think he's useful. Then you waited interminably for the old man to tie it up, his motions slow and spasmodic. It was serious work, terrifically solid, with crooked knots requiring a pocketknife to loosen; his hands knew exactly what they were doing but his head was empty. So you would compliment him on his hands: That's

126

so beautiful; that's so sturdy; that's so neat. The head didn't answer. You would take back your package and the hands just kept on moving, tying perfect packages in the void.

Inside the package Victor unfolded small, humiliated pieces of paper showing tears from Scotch tape even though it had been unstuck very carefully, worn papers, papers broken by the corners of other presents. Papers put away carefully by old people who have never had anything, the same way others put away sheets, rags, napkins – nice and flat in a chest of drawers. Pieces of paper she had ironed earlier. Papers from Victor's childhood – all part of his history. He remembered a game of little horses, a gift received in the red paper printed with Christmas trees and balls. In the tissue paper that used to keep his black armband safe, the gold paper in which Rozan chocolates used to be wrapped . . . He found a bib embroidered with "baby" in big, raised letters that imitated English script, a cup with "Victor" engraved on it, and the silver so worn off that you could see the yellowed metal behind it, and a frilly undershirt his grandmother said was for a toddler. These are your things, she explained, she had put them together in a great rush. The Misses Favre had already started making him something because at this age children grow fast.

Less, however, than she thinks, Victor remarked as he put his undershirt on the monkey, a foot and a half too long in the arms; the bib was like a halter top. There was nothing that could have made him less human and more a monkey. Oh, how pretty he is! Queen Mab exclaimed. She had had her eye on the store and run right over as soon as she'd heard a package had come – just in case there was something she could make off with. How very pretty Mr. Alexis is like that, wearing that handsome suit; because it isn't right, she said sententiously, for the son of Babel to go around in a hair coat. You will clothe your nakedness for nakedness is corrupted by sin. The monkey curled his lips and showed his teeth;

he was on all fours facing Queen Mab, growling like a mastiff, an animal, horribly.

When she saw the cup the gigantic woman's eyes began to sparkle. She blinked and reached out; she wanted to pretend that she wasn't seeing or touching anything but she was all eye, all hand. The gleaming cup was irresistible to her. What is that? she asked, feigning indifference. My cup, he said. When she heard his "my," she figured that he would be in no hurry to let go of it; so, being a good businesswoman, she didn't offer a price.

The monkey, bundled tightly in clothes, was in a rage; he pulled at the bib, flung his arms about. Getting Victor's childhood dirty . . . It was all too overwhelming. Unexpectedly, but luckily, César's car stopped in front of the Resource. Did Victor want anything, Lola called from the car door; she was going to Port-Banane. Nothing, he replied testily. She saw the monkey and burst out laughing. He's funny, she said. Victor didn't hear what she said and made her repeat it. He's funny with that on; she pointed to the bib. Victor shrugged his shoulders.

Queen Mab couldn't manage to leave; she was afraid that if she left the cup would disappear. That's a beautiful woman, she remarked, pointing her thumb at the car driving off; a little kowtowing wouldn't hurt her. That woman is for you, not for the old man. She had gone too far. She was stirring up something incredibly sensitive and painful. Get out of here, he told her. She let the storm blow over. She eyed the cup with such intensity that B and B, staring wide-eyed, could literally see what she saw: a ciborium to hold the Sacrament on an altar, a ciborium for Brother Emmanuel, the one who was her own true love.

By evening she had still not begun to negotiate. Conversation dragged on and became more confiding; they discussed how hard it was to do business and she told him what she did when she worked in the canteen. Never serve anything without taking a spoonful of it. Twenty servings at twenty spoonfuls, you've got one more serving. In twenty days you have twenty more servings. You want to get everything at once, do big business, because you don't like it. Real pleasure comes from little things. I earn more than you do, she told him, and I don't have all of this. She gestured toward the Resource but ended up with her index finger pointing straight at the cup in spite of herself. The monkey had finally pulled his bib off. B and B lit the lights and the cup sparkled on the counter. How much? she said abruptly.

They heard the sound of a car's brakes. Lola breezed in; she was so blond, so blond that Victor was speechless. Here, she said to him, I brought something, it's for Alexis. In a little plastic box there was a medal. It's just plated, she apologized: a little round, curly-haired cherub looking pensively at the universe, his chin cradled in his hand. A medal that was the picture of the cozy, precious child-hood, with dimples meant to be kissed, that nobody there, not a single one of them – the Humpback, the Cripple, Queen Mab, Victor, Lola – ever knew. They thought about childhood the same way you'd think about angels: a perfection you don't see yourself as part of. Great, ethereal creatures with immense wings who were unaffected by earthly burdens; they keep a vague watch but are always going off to brandish their firearms and play war games with each other, games they have copied from the knights.

They pinned the medal on the monkey's shirt, decorated him with childhood. Baby in the morning, he was an angel at night; monkeys don't go by the same time as we do. And, comparing him to the image, all anyone could say was that he looked even less like an angel than a human. Pale and hairy in the bottom of his box, he was all of creation – humiliated. You are beautiful, said Lola, and her white hands sank into the dark abundant hair she was caress-ing. The monkey grabbed one of her hairs with his frantic fingers, a golden thread that he pulled out.

Looking at them side by side Victor realized that the angel was the woman, an angel from a golden medal, fixed in place by the precious matter covering her like a thin layer; it closed her mouth, her nose and eyes, the hand supporting her chin right above the monkey's box, as if she had fallen into a bath of gold and it had killed her.

The Dreadnought

Monkey time was not the same as human time. His grandmother's letters, which made their difficult way to him month after month, made this obvious. At first Alexis had been far more advanced than she imagined, even more advanced than Victor as an infant when, good baby, he spent long hours in his cradle sucking on a bit of flannel blanket. All the monkey's teeth had come in at once, arming his thick jaw with fanglike canines whenever he curled his lips. Back home they imagined him sucking dreamily on a rubber pacifier dipped in honey. He walked very fast, agile as a dancer, spinning and twirling before human babies even summoned the strength to lift their heads. And Victor, confronted with the monkey, mused over the pathetic childhood of humans, their imperfect bodies, the way they moved like awkward insects. The monkey's curiosity never quit; he searched everything, he turned the door handles, he liked to open and close drawers and see how liquid came out of bottles.

But when the others began to talk you could see he was well behind. To make himself understood he only had a series of yelps emitted through disproportionately elongated lips to express love, curiosity, desire, and satisfaction, and an acrimonious, jaw-exposing screech to vent fear and rage. And in between – nothing – no voice came out. When toddlers would have been inflecting their laughter, lisping nursery rhymes, making up words, he could do none of it. His voice had set up like concrete in his throat, where time would turn it into gravel. His voice changed prematurely, deadening it horribly; it transformed the charming creature into a brute. An animal is a human whose voice changes too soon. He wasn't going to speak, he would never speak.

His eyes, too, astonished, unblinking, held wide open by a stupid, crude dream, remained stuck in animality. Dull eyes with a completely invasive iris, at the back of which there was a pinpoint of a pupil – no light in them other than what they reflected, taking on reddish, brownish, or mud-colored tints, depending on what was nearby; when Lola drew her blond head close they reflected all the glitter of gold – which was taken to be joy. The monkey felt sadness without tears, happiness with no emotion. When sleep came he lowered his rubbery lids, thicker than human eyelids – longer too.

The monkey returned to his true nature when he descended into sleep as if going back into a cave or a chasm. He only indulged in brief naps, light sleep, part of his instinct always alert for sounds, and a shadow would wake him up. Lively as a spring, he would bounce back to life. Instantly up on all four feet, his ugly mug low to the ground, looking for food, sniffing his bowl, his lower lip stuck out to drink water straight from a puddle. All the human ways of doing things forgotten, erased as he slept. He had to start from scratch. A brute that collected and sniffed and then dumped its feces right where it was with no respect for decency. Victor used to find it tasting its excrement, squashing its turds. It was filthy and stank of all its resurgent animality.

It was about that time that his grandmother, remembering what an adorable little boy he had been, sent him a sailor suit stamped *The Dreadnought* that she had coveted so much on one of the Favre children that they had finally given it to her. You only wore it one time, she stressed. Yes, just once, to go thank the Misses Favre who were so nice. He had been a complete success; it was the first time he had worn big boy's clothes. They turned him round and around, they had examined him from every angle. The pants were attached to the blouse by a series of buttons that didn't stay on very well. And it was one of the Misses Favre who sewed them back on. That spinster lady had come right up and touched him, bent down over his waist and sewed "solid." I was dying of shame, his grandmother recalled. The lady had a false chignon differing by two or three shades from her hair color. He had wanted to touch it where it changed color. When he was all sewn up again, The Dreadnought was gone, enclosed.

A monkey several months old is much more slender than a child the same age; without the buttons he would have lost his britches. Alexis went into a tizzy: he struggled when they put the clothes on but then took off at breakneck speed to display himself in front of the store. Queen Mab was flabbergasted. Her first impulse was to run over and see close up, but she decided that an attitude of indifference would be more becoming to her dignity. The monkey bounced like a spring and screeched in falsetto; he looked like a mechanical toy wound so tight that it repeats the same action over and over until you just can't watch it any more.

In a twinkling everyone in the village knew and the women came to see; they liked the monkey better this way than covered with hair. He definitely looked like a white person, which made everybody feel happier. The monkey howled with fear when it saw the great crowd of people; he sounded like a dog going hoarse. Dashing between Victor's legs, he hobbled him so he couldn't move, couldn't get anywhere. Victor wanted to shout at them to go away and leave him alone.

But he restrained himself because of the children. The first result of Gilbert's retaliation had been that school had been abolished and Clément dismissed, sent back to his library. The children had been roaming around ever since. They were delighted by Alexis. They would sit in the dust and wait – just like at a puppet show – to see Alexis come out and play the clown; they made faces back at him so he became ten times as excited. But when they saw him wearing the *Dreadnought* uniform, spinning the sailor's hat like a hoop, they stopped laughing. They understood that Alexis was a superior being, one who could have white and gold outfits, one authorized to wear a uniform. The little uniform introduced the cycle of envy and frustration to this place; wealth now thumbed its nose at poverty. And Victor wanted to hit the strutting monkey; a frantic need to give the children something swept over him. He looked all around, but all he saw was swollen cans, bags of rot, pressure cookers.

Can Alexis come play with us, Mister? one of the little kids asked very politely. Alexis, do you want to go play with the children? Alexis pouted prettily, pretended to be shy, but he was happy. He held onto Victor's legs with his forearms and waddled from side to side waggling his hindquarters – irrefutable proof of great joy. I'll take off his clothes, Victor told the children, the way you talk about a little boy invited to a party: he has to get ready. No, Mister, said one little girl, leave him like that, all pretty and everything, we promise, he won't get dirty. Victor consented and gave them some final advice: Don't take him too far, don't get rough, don't play ball . . . And then he bent down to Alexis, took him in his arms, gave him a kiss, and told him to have a nice afternoon, the way his grandmother used to do at times like this.

Alexis went off, one child on either side holding his hands; he was still little and his long arms were held straight up to reach the children's hands. Victor wanted to ask them to carry him because his legs were short, but a child caught his eye, a baby at the tail end of the group, who had barely learned to walk and was scampering along the best he could behind them with the faltering, perilous gait of a toddler; he wanted to see the monkey. But he, the little boy, was naked, with a fat belly on two pitiful, spindly, little legs. So Victor went back to his business.

Alexis had decided to be friends with the little girl and then took a liking to each of the children in turn, provided they didn't touch him too much; he was ticklish. They went through the village, a wretched, ragged horde full of chatter. Undecided as to what to play, arguing over the best thing to do, wanting to celebrate such an extraordinary event. Not soccer, not four corners, not a race . . . So why not hot-bat? Do you know how to play hot-bat, Alexis? the little girl asked maternally. She gravely declared to the group that hot-bat was the favorite pastime of *The Dreadnought*.

They flushed and caught a bat, soft as a ripe fig on a stalk. The prisoner struggled a bit. The children screamed; it got away and flew low to the ground; they caught it again. They put a string on its foot and dragged it the whole length of the road like a little ball; it bounced off every rock. They looked for some spikes and found a carpenter's nail, thick and crooked, covered with such thick rust that it had, you might say, formed new parts; and with some barbed wire they managed to fabricate something more or less pointed. They nailed the animal on the school door. The big nail tore the bat's fragile wing membrane and the little creature fell. They picked it up and fastened it through both sides of the webbing at once, right at the joint. Look, Alexis, look, my darling, said the little girl, her eyes sparkling with pleasure.

Alexis seemed interested by the little crucified form throbbing with pain. Then one of the big boys lit a cigarette made of grass rolled up in a dried banana leaf; he took a few puffs and then put the cigarette in the bat's mouth. The animal panted so from suffering that you could clearly see the tip of the cigarette blaze with each breath in and smoke rise with each breath out. It's smoking, it's smoking, shouted the children. Pain made the little creature breathe faster and faster, and to accompany its suffocation the children shouted louder and louder, faster and faster, until there was a little glowing tip in its mouth, until its mouth stretched wide around the flame, until it caught completely on fire . . . My darling, my darling, chanted the little girl, did you see the hot bat? And she gave the monkey a zesty kiss.

The Savage Heart

And finally, after all this, Brother Emmanuel's heart went wild. Every time he woke up a spasm of disgust for mankind came over him. He felt sick, sad, and spiteful. He closed his eyes and put his hands together; Queen Mab said he was saying his prayers and was not to be disturbed. She wouldn't light a lamp or make any noise because if she did he exploded into horrific rage. All this evil bubbling up tore him apart. He tossed and turned, flailed his arms, kicked his feet; his eyes bugged out and on top of it all he screamed loudly, bellowing things nobody understood. People misjudged the symptoms; they were afraid of being hit or maybe killed; they couldn't see that Brother Emmanuel was in pain.

But Queen Mab knew. She wrapped her large arms and legs around him and struggle as he might against her fat stomach and huge breast, it amounted to no more than the wiggles of an infant and he grew calm. Only then did she speak to him: Shall we read something from the Scriptures? He nodded his agreement, like a small child, still upset but seeing through his misery the promise of being comforted and feeling already that his grief is sweet.

She loosened her hair and took off all the little shells at the ends of her innumerable braids; she put them into the hollow of his hand. Sitting in the dust he rolled them out as anxiously and briskly as a gambler feverishly throwing dice. They counted the shells' pink undersides to decide which page and their iridescent backs to decide which verse. She opened Father Jean's book and read what fate had specified. Brother Emmanuel expected God would order him to leave but there was still nothing in the book about that. It was all just damnation and war. God was displeased and called them a stiff-necked people. God did not love them.

He gave her back the little shells and watched her fix her hair again, smoothing the tip of each braid with a bit of spit so she could slip the shells on, knotting them into her hair like little bells, pulling all the braids up together and attaching them on the top of her head, and finally wrapping her magical head with a huge turban. She did her very best to comfort him. She told him that he must not be impatient with fate: since all had been written, all would take place. He answered that he knew all that but his doubts were about himself; he wondered if on the day the commandment came he would still be strong enough to leave. She replied that God had certainly brought Moses out of Egypt land, from the house of slaves, that God had brought him through the great and dreadful desert in the midst of burning snakes and implacable scorpions . . .

Scripture calmed Emmanuel; Queen Mab's lips were cut out for letting the Word pass through them. It was like a spring flowing between two rocks polished by the clear water. He watched her mouth when she read or spoke the way you watch a spring welling up, seeing how it changes but never changes. All other mouths he hated: white women's red mouths, mouths discussing everyday matters, mouths that laugh. He loved Queen Mab's mouth and also the nontalking mouth of the monkey.

But no matter how hard she tried to reassure him, Queen Mab's heart was sad. She knew he was going to leave, that she would not keep him there by playing with shells in the sand, with stories of blood and gold. Anything she might do to keep him would take away his happiness and make him bitter. His desire to leave was now so strong that he would go without God's blessing – without her blessing – which was the same thing. He would take off running, and that would be a great catastrophe, as if God's will had actually foundered.

She stroked the big body stretched out beside her; she stroked his back, which had now grown broader, and his hard belly; gently, dreamily she stroked his cheeks but he kept his face down. He preferred the cold earth to her large thighs, hot beneath the purple silk skirt. He withdrew into himself. She could tell that her own body could go no farther, get no larger, no fatter, no more solid in order to wed this child's body hardening in despair. She could do no more. She had given birth to the sky but no longer had the strength to bring the water and fish of the sea into the world. He was bound to leave.

She promised (though she didn't believe it) that there was some little one without a name he could baptize. What shall we call him? He knew this was just a promise, a tidbit she was tossing him. There were no baptisms in the offing, but she had every intention of finding him one in no time flat even if she had to push on some woman's belly to bring to light a lingering fetus. He shook his head; he'd rather stay here on the ground next to this woman he was divorcing. Look at me, she said. He refused to turn his eyes in her direction. Look at me, she insisted, and put her hands to her mouth as she discovered what she dreaded: Emmanuel's eyes were filled with a liquid, desperate darkness.

It was her fault, too: always talking paradise – paradise here, paradise there – so that finally he believed it and in the end he didn't have it; he wanted paradise instantly. What's written is written. Period, end of story. It was simple: there had once been paradise, then came the fall, then comes paradise. In between there's sin and reparation. He had sinned, gone astray and sinned, and now he wanted to return. Period, end of story. He had been given the task of converting the faithful to make amends for sin. All he knew was that he was not returning all alone. Queen Mab agreed about everything except his returning. She was scared stiff of that. For herself she was in no hurry. I have my own mission, she said. Brother Emmanuel had a strong suspicion that her mission was to sell things through the Resource. She wanted to be the big businesswoman in Africa.

His own paradise had a prodigious flavor of childhood. He would have been able to locate it on a map – precisely under the tree where the village held its never-ending discussions. In the rainy season the tree was huge and red as flame and in the dry months it was lush and green. Hens scratched there in the dust and lizards with their throbbing throats and yellow bodies pursued their little gray females. He also saw a dog, a bitch, lying on her side, her pink teats spread out on the sand. Paradise – it was there, between the legs of the men waving fly-chasers, between the arms of the women who would grab the children racing past them and proceed to delouse a little one. Paradise – he could have put a date on it, too: it took place before he was fifteen, before Father Jean had come, in the days of the veteran who used to tell some very interesting stories punctuated by noisy throat clearing. A few sighs when he got too out of breath.

Then there was the flight, the mucus, tears, and blood on his fingers and sobs in his throat: that was the fall. Nothing, not a word, the little book shut up tight as a stone. He was a man who had carried a book through the forest. He had often wanted to toss it along with Father Jean's knapsack and crucifix, but he had kept it because, otherwise, his hands would have closed around nothing, his shoulders would have carried nothing, and his arms would have held nothing. It was the book that had kept him human through the ordeal. Without the book his arms would have grown longer and his hands shriveled up like horseshoes on a mare's hooves.

And then he had had to learn about the world, not the world of the village with its ground millet or manioc, the sauce of greens cooked forever and spicy with hot peppers – the other world, the one completely infected with savagery that humans don't even remember because they haven't given it a name. All he had for dealing with unknown fruits were smell and taste; his nose and mouth struggled to understand which were good and which bad. Nature played terrible tricks: sweet things were not always good nor stinking things bad. Such and such a pod, fleshy and sweet, had dealt him a blow in the stomach like violent poison; such and such a fruit, bitter and fetid, had cured him. His eyes looked past appearances, his ears heard below the level of sound. He was threatened by everything; only his filth was kindly and good, but the animals, the flies, and the ants fought him over it.

He had become a man when he had rediscovered his place among the animals and in nature. His beard grew the way it does on explorers lost in the virgin forest and only discovered years later, ghosts of themselves; his beard grew the way hair turns white all of a sudden because the ordeal was too harsh. Then, a few unsteady steps and there was a tree he didn't know with a long fruit that didn't make him sick, a forest of these trees, water that flowed at midday. He had spent a year in the banana plantation without being afraid of the big monkeys that came as he did to the edge of the forest to gather a supply of bananas and water. He and the monkeys watched the men go by, running beneath their burden; they watched in silence, dumbfounded, terrified by these humans whereas they had no fear of each other. This is how it went until Queen Mab recognized him by the side of the well and told him the meaning of the book.

The village gave him comfort and power, speech and writing. He could have set himself up in what Queen Mab called happiness. He, too, could have tried to get hold of the Resource and with her become the big businessman of Africa. But that was where they differed, happiness did not satisfy him, he was clogged with uneasiness, bristling with anxieties, preoccupied with one desire that took a long time to reveal itself, then to take shape and become a necessity. It was basically nothing but the desire to return to paradise, which, of course, had made Queen Mab shrug her fat shoulders and now, he could easily tell from the smell and color of her flesh, from the way she had fixed her hair again, was making her very sad.

She took out her bad humor on Victor. She demanded abruptly that he pay her back. Give me what you have, she told him. But I don't have anything, he replied, beside himself. Give it to me, she persisted, dollars, pounds, marks, yens . . . I don't have anything, nothing, nothing. Gold watch, silver, jewels? I don't have anything; he emptied what was in his pockets out onto the counter. And that? she said to him as she ogled his wallet. He opened it to show her; he took out his identification papers, the dreadful contract binding him to the Resource. A small piece of tissue paper fell out. He had forgotten the garnets set in earrings. They were tiny, black as rat droppings. Those, she said. I can't, he replied. Why? she asked. Because . . . Give me them, she demanded, and he gave her the earrings. I'll come back tomorrow, she told him as she screwed the dangles onto her ears, and you'll pay your debt. I can't wait anymore, either.

The Magnificent

They had a day off after shipment of the Little Green Dwarves and before the Large Yellow Dwarves were to go out, so services were held at Queen Mab's. Brother Emmanuel put on a lace petticoat with its seams slit open for his arms. Queen Mab cleared the table. Into two Vittel water bottles cut off below the neck she put some flowers – herbaceous plants: chickpeas in bloom and lush with seeds, mustard yellow. The only flowers that grew here, their appearance in itself represented the swift passage of time. So that one of the faithful who fell asleep at the beginning of the service would have been able to imagine, by the way the stalks were leaning and by how dry the leaves were, that the mass had gone on for a week, whereas they were just barely beginning: on the road to paradise.

It was a religion as unchanging as the climate at the Devil, no sacrifices, no feast days, no seasons, and no days of remembrance – a religion intent on just one promise, just one hope. Surrounded by the bouquets of flowers, Brother Emmanuel would endlessly repeat the Word chosen by Queen Mab and the others picked it up ecstatically in chorus. Victor heard them the way he heard the schoolchildren, the way he heard the workers in the drying plant or the huge sprinklers that made it rain on the banana trees. It was a mechanical sound like the one a saw makes; you forget it while it's going on and then, when it stops, you notice through the stupor of silence that its whine had almost made you sick. This is what life is like in prisons, he thought. He understood why Guastavin had been obsessed with weather reports.

But César, up there on the terrace of his house, crossed his little legs, blinked his eyes at the curtain of rain, and turned to speak to Gilbert, who was living with him now that Lola was gone. He said: The terrific thing here is that nothing will ever change. He was comfortable there with this twin brother, who was younger, handsomer, and more enterprising – the precise image of what he had been, as if, with Gilbert beside him, his youth was bound to stay with him eternally. They set their watches together, agreeing on the hour, the same exact minute, the same exact second; they set their hearts together.

Gilbert wanted to be done with it: now that Clément and Lola were gone, he wanted to dismiss the priest. César was doing his best to convince him that this outward show of religion had given the village its cohesiveness. He hadn't forbidden it despite the orders of Guastavin, who claimed that it disrupted the next day's work, that the workers were less supple, more full of protest, worse loudmouths. In the beginning, before Brother Emmanuel, their day off was a day when memories returned with nostalgia; you would see them wandering up and down the two roads crossing at right angles; they wanted beer to drink and herbs to chew and smoke . . . Whereas now they put on white loincloths and the women wove thin strips of banana leaves into their hair. It looked clean. Think about it, my dear Gilbert. But as far as Gilbert was concerned, he'd done enough thinking about it.

They had the Word, but not the formula for the Word. They wandered tirelessly, crudely, and blindly through the texts. They didn't understand. They understood nothing, as if the light had been abruptly turned off. They were in the dark. Lost and scared, they would sometimes see a word as a glimmer showing the way out. They would race for it and smash their faces on a sheer wall, the base of a cliff. It was rarely an important word, just one floating around everywhere, a little word meant for people like them – people without hope, without knowledge. They, on the other hand, immediately recognized the Word exploding there, from threats to curses, God's anger and despair as if it had been shouted in their ears.

Called a race of vipers, they asked forgiveness. Accused of being spreaders of iniquity, they asked forgiveness; compared to a tree cut down and thrown into the fire, they asked forgiveness; they were told they were sterile land as hard as a rock and they agreed and asked forgiveness. They had been told: convert, for the kingdom of heaven is at hand; they converted. They had been threatened with hell and Gehenna, flames and remorse, and they were waiting for hell and Gehenna, flames and remorse. Because it's just as hard to be chosen as it is to be damned.

Then Queen Mab had set up the altar; between the two bouquets she placed the silver cup. Magnificent in all her veils, she went to sit down; she was wearing an excess of purple, a great flowing boubou, a turban of satin brocade; she was wearing all her jewelry, a necklace of gold coins from France, bracelets of dollars, and the garnet earrings. Silently they waited for her to open the book. Emmanuel closed his eyes, clenched his fists. Way deep inside he knew that if the order to leave was still denied him he wouldn't stand for it. He didn't know what he would say or do but he wouldn't stand for it. Queen Mab's fingers moved speculatively along the edge of the book; she opened it. She read God's commandment.

Brother Emmanuel's mouth opened and joy made words of milk and honey flow from his lips, and in the midst of all these sweet and strong words spilling onto their heads, the men, women, and children who were there heard the word *magnificent, you are magnificent* ... They hadn't understood the rest but *magnificent*, called out like that and repeated by Brother Emmanuel over and over and over, as usual, then modulated, chanted, was dazzling. The word in itself was a glorious song. Now they saw that they were magnificent and they expected to be called magnificent.

The Word had become comforting and benevolent. After hell it was promising paradise. Take us into a good land, Queen Mab began to sing in her beautiful voice – resonant, so warm, so ardent that sweat sprayed in their faces, a land of torrents, springs and streams bubbling up in the valleys and on the mountains. We shall go to the promised land, the crowd repeated. And, to put more power into her voice, Queen Mab closed her eyes: We shall go through the great forest, we shall go through the vast river. We shall take the road to paradise, the crowd shouted in a single voice, we shall find the land of our birth. We shall break our chains, we shall break the shackles on our voices. Queen Mab was big and beautiful; it was as if the song had totally fulfilled her. We shall go, we shall go, chanted the crowd; already the women were crying. We shall bless each stone in the path, we shall glorify every green thing in the earth, and we shall name the birds in your heavens ... We shall go, we shall go, moaned the crowd, and the men were sobbing. So peace took a firm hold in Emmanuel's heart.

Back at African Resource Victor was in the shade figuring out just how much he owed Queen Mab – an enormous amount, of which he had not a single penny. He would have to sell the stock – the only improvement he could lay claim to – or he was bankrupt. Fear loosened its grip and he began to feel a sort of relief in the face of this dreaded catastrophe, as if, now that what was fated had come to pass, he could glimpse his freedom in this failure. Still holding the ballpoint pen, he stopped adding up figures; he thought he heard very pure voices, something like a magnificat sung inside a stone cloister. He thought of his grandmother; he thought of Lola, whom he hadn't seen for quite some while. He thought with no regrets, no sorrow; it was all screwed up with them as well. He went to find the monkey, took him in his arms, and went to the window to see the crowd go its separate ways; but today the services seemed to go on longer than usual.

144

Queen Mab, extremely large, extremely beautiful, stood up. The garnets sparkled on her ears like too-long reddish flames consuming her face. She lifted the cloth covering the altar and Emmanuel recognized the boxes. He shivered. How would I have managed without you? he asked her. But he said it just for the sake of form; he no longer needed Queen Mab. Very gravely, very sincerely she replied to him under her breath so no one could hear: Your path lies open in your heart. He vaguely protested. And you know what the Word says. I can't do without you, he said, but she didn't believe him. I'll follow you wherever you go, she replied, but he didn't believe her. They were divorced.

Queen Mab sat next to the altar. The faithful came forward one after the other, silent, calm, and serene; they put out their hands and Emmanuel gave them the white powder; they crossed themselves and put everything they owned – crumpled bills, flimsy little coins, gold fragments – into Queen Mab's vast skirt, between her spread thighs. They had obtained what was essential; they were getting rid of the useless and superfluous things. But there was nothing, as far as she was concerned, that would pay for the loss she was suffering.

Victor saw Queen Mab at the end of the road, near where Guastavin's house had been torn down. The folds of her vast robe moved like waves on the sea, her floating veil trapped all the wind. He saw her silhouette grow larger before his eyes; she was only twenty yards away, ten, she was there in front of him, enormous, straight, and tall as she could be, hands on her hips. She was wearing his grandmother's garnets; he didn't remember the earrings being so long, so rich, tongues of flame.

I have *nothing!* he cried.

So I'm taking the Resource, she said. Instantly, Victor saw the money to go home, the money to marry Lola, the money to provide his grandmother with a living. He was fixing up the house, enlarging the garden. On Sundays he would go to the village square with Lola on his arm and Alexis holding his hand. His grandmother would watch them from the window. Yes, he said. He expected a tremendous sum. Poker. Queen Mab opened her skirt, spread out the money given by the faithful. So much, so much. She chose two bills and handed them to Victor. Here, she said.

But, he said, that's nothing! It was roughly enough to pay for one ticket, in steerage at that, and only if he swept and peeled day and night. And Lola? he said. How am I going to take Lola? She's at the Sunset, your Lola. She's a big whore, your Lady. Also, she said, you're taking the monkey. I don't want any monkeys in the store. Monkeys are not my kind of thing. You've got twenty-four hours, she added; B and B will come get the key tomorrow morning.

Go Home

Victor went off toward the planter's house. The night was filled with winged rhythms, with cloying, sweet caws, with slippery, elusive crawling. The entire banana plantation sighed and moaned, gasping for breath. He was part of the shadows, part of their blind swarming, caught in the magma of creation and mud, awaiting some action that would throw him out into the very pure light of the night. An animal caught sight of the moon and stars and gave a great shout of joy already hoarsening into death. And Victor, looking way off into the darkness where he sought the light of her pale hair on the terrace, didn't see it and felt his heart burn with such intensity that he, like an animal, could have cried out to death. And death wasn't all that far away, like a journey from which you never return.

He went back to the Resource. He took Alexis in his arms and Alexis, as usual, hung on. Victor wandered around the store in the midst of unsold articles – irons, toasters, bras – looking for something to eat. The can of sardines was still prominently displayed. He opened it as well as a can of milk he was keeping in case Alexis got sick, and there on the counter they ate together with their fingers. The food wasn't as good as they had hoped. Outside something was going on: the same rustling and creaking sounds that he had heard the first evening at Guastavin's. He made sure everything was closed up tight. The Resource was sealed off; no air came in and, surrounded by all the stuff, it was suffocating. Nonetheless he lay down and the monkey nestled up against him. Victor loved the strong smell of the monkey's body touching his, its rough fur. He pricked up his ears: there was less noise. All you could hear in the warehouse was the sound of Alexis's lips sucking on the empty can. If I make it through all this, Victor thought as he fell asleep, if I pull through, I'm leaving.

When he woke up the village was empty. He raised the iron blinds and saw B and B wearing large hats and jogging down the deserted road toward him. They had come to clean: they had to have water, soap, mops. But the whole time I've been here you've done nothing, said Victor in astonishment. Because you never asked us to do anything, they replied. Victor blew up: That's not true! He reminded them of how they were always complaining. Maybe, but you never insisted. Victor thought they looked strange: their faces were pink and their hair was now blond. They were angelic and, at the same time, revolting. Hand over the key, they demanded.

Victor rolled his remaining possessions up in a sheet: the ballpoint pen and the bit of soap. In addition he took a toaster and an iron, then he put on his black suit. He thought it looked faded and white everywhere he had perspired – under his arms, on his back, in his groin. He wiped it off, which left green spots. The monkey climbed onto his back and they set off. Victor walked

147

swiftly; he wanted to get back on the road as quickly as possible, put his shoes on, find a car, hitchhike.

Finally he saw macadam, like a black, solidified flow of lava on the red dirt road. They passed alongside a line of army trucks. The soldiers packed in under the canvas covers were amusing themselves by trying on gas masks. Only too glad to meet up with a passerby, they showed off their Martian faces. When he got as far as the first Jeeps, their radio antennas up and crackling bravos, tangos, charlies, Victor found somebody with some information. What was going on? Eight hundred people had vanished in thin air, the eight hundred workers from Devil's Banana. The men were waiting for helicopter reinforcements in order to pursue the investigation. Victor said that, in fact, he was coming from Devil's Banana. They kept him there: what he had witnessed might be of interest. An officer proposed taking him to the high command in Mégalo.

The officer had a straight, short nose, above which jutted a straight, short visor like some redundant proboscis. He was part of the new generation with plenty of intellectual baggage; when the older men talked about war he had the word peace on his lips. He respected the local populations and tried hard to learn their dialects. He had an ideal and firm convictions; he believed in communication and used psychology. He was ready to begin some delicate negotiations when Victor – with his long, blond hair, his monkey on his shoulder, his black suit and bare feet, resembling him in age, country, culture, and language – had happened by, but he didn't know how to talk to this man. The lieutenant with the short, straight nose was courteous and managed to overcome his natural repugnance for the individual he was escorting. He didn't want to begin a conversation but made a few rumbling noises. Then words came and he heard himself talking like the old soldiers, those men he didn't want to be like. He surprised himself by saying things he had never thought in words he had never used. He was troubled by the warlike onomatopoeias belonging to distant, forgotten battles that came out of his mouth.

To cover up his distress he pretended to be interested in Alexis; he asked his age. Like a dung beetle rolling its ball his mind was kneading all sorts of monstrous and unspeakable things together. He began with some reflections on monkeys who turn violent, especially – when they become adult – with women and then, against his will, he veered off into a story he had once heard: a rape, a gorilla, and a *negress!* There, he'd said it! Usually very discreet and, like everyone of his generation, displaying great scorn for the tales told in the barracks, he was ashamed of the image he was presenting. But Victor was not overly struck by it; he didn't imagine that a soldier whose rank he couldn't quite tell would have been able to express himself any differently. He was just wondering what would happen to the handsome lieutenant if one day he broke his nose, if, in place of the thin, straight bridge there was a round schnozzle, a snout. He thought of how fragile human attitudes were; if the nose were off what would remain of the fine convictions and no less fine hopes of this captain, excuse me, of this lieutenant?

Mégalo opened itself to the visitor through a series of concentric circles; the city had grown like a tree in successive rings of expansion. They had gone through the suburbs, as the officer, who had now pulled himself together, called them. Monkey, monkey, the idea grew larger and larger, a ball of shit lifting him; it was enormous, ready to explode. On top of it, his arms crossed, incapable of holding it in: Monkey, he finally said, is what we used to *eat* in Indochina. And, since Victor didn't understand: Monkey is their corned beef! Oof, he restrained himself at the last minute.

They reached the center where the park was as well as the villas of former government officials and the consulates and the chic cafés. They went into the embassy, passing between two soldiers wearing helmets, white gaiters, and gloves who presented arms to the lieutenant and consequently to Victor and consequently to the monkey. Two or three corridors, desks, women who stuck their heads out to watch them go by and give little squeals when they caught sight of Alexis. *Here*, said the lieutenant and stopped himself just in time; he was about to shout, *Down!* Through the half-open door Victor could vaguely hear that they had found a guy on the road who was all screwed up, some "bloke." The lieutenant was sufficiently agitated that his superior in rank asked him if "everything" was going well. Distraught, the lieutenant wiped his handsome face: I don't know anymore, he said, it's this fellow and his monkey . . .

Victor took advantage of the moment to put his shoes on. His feet had grown thicker and the shoes pinched. Alexis amused himself with the laces, trying to get them to go through the holes. Finally they came to get him; he was able to testify about everything he knew – in other words, he said he knew nothing. They asked him if there hadn't been anything at all abnormal recently. *Abnormal?* Victor repeated, turning the word over in his mind. Suddenly he understood and wanted to laugh. *Monkey*, said the lieutenant, extremely pale. There were *monkey tables*. They would put the head of a monkey into a vice. Crack, they opened it up like an egg. Victor laughed. Yes, yes, the lieutenant contended, thinking it was a skeptical laugh. You had to eat while it was hot; the paws and arms wiggled around under the table. Retching over his own description, the lieutenant left the room. In the captain's office the lieutenant complained about his head; no, this was no ordinary migraine but a consuming light that was burning him like tongues of fire and he was mixing all the words up, all the words . . .

Abnormal? Victor laughed until he cried. After they had made him state his name, age, job, profession, address, and intentions, they asked him what he had seen. Nothing, he said. They let him go. Victor wondered how he was going to get across the road, teeming with people this time of day, so he could make himself comfortable in the Toucan Bar with its cold drinks and air conditioner. Which door did you have to push? The clients, all white and, with rare exceptions, all men, were behind a window and from the sidewalk you could feel how cool and refreshed they were. Victor was with all the guys on the sidewalk looking into the aquarium. Outside with all the souvenir sellers, shoe polishers, and child taxis. Waiting there with all the lame men, the blind beggars, the lepers from the post office, and the legless cripple from the supermarket, all of them competing. He held the monkey by the hand and the other men, the ones on the sidewalk, had made a little room for him; the monkey was his disability. And the others, the men in the aquarium, let the same absentminded gaze sweep over him; they were used to not seeing the wounds, snakes with their mouths torn off, parrots with dried-up feet, mongooses with their eyes gouged out. He was white and he wasn't white anymore because he had the monkey. So they left.

The Blessed

The village had emptied out overnight; the coolies had taken off. They had marched straight ahead through roads opened to harvest the bananas. Silence. They would not speak until they were out of the banana plantation. They could hear the slight, distant crackle of the insecticide plane in the sky, above the leaves. They were racing to get out of the banana plantation before it released the bug-killing phosphorus. And the little plane went along happily through the sky; it looped loops and dove as if drunk on the chemical it was carrying. This was no careful, systematic sweeping like when it distributed the chemical in long, narrow lines to kill vermin; this was bombardment and the aviator in his old crate felt decidedly warlike – the same feeling he might have felt fifty years earlier dropping real bombs. What he wanted to see was *them* coming out of their hole, all smoked out. Objective attained. Mission accomplished. He raised his index finger and thumb to signal A-OK. Request permission to return. Return granted. Successful landing. A chick on each arm. Champagne at the squadron bar.

Except *they* were not under the banana trees; they were already in the mangrove. The water and land mingled under the gigantic roots of the mangrove trees; water, but not water: thick and heavy; land, but not land: light and flowing through your fingers. And there, like the catfish, the web-footed lizards and the sea toads, the weakest, the sick, and the old asked to remain. Crossing the banana plantation at breakneck speed had exhausted them. They thought this water, land, and mud were fine. A good enough paradise to suit them. We have everything here, they said. At night they would climb up into the trees with the snakes that had feet and the birds that had fins. But Emmanuel, fortified by his victory over the airplane, ordered them to carry on. He told them the place was not yet human and they had to wait for when the land would be divided from the waters.

In the morning they saw the water of the river – calm, flat, fresh water. It was so transparent along the banks that you could see the pebbles glistening. If water of the earth was like that what would the purifying water be like? And faced with this beauty they stood up straight again, rooted to the spot out of respect for creation and pride in it. They had a sharp and sudden sense of the painful humiliations they had suffered. They stayed there on the shore watching the river awaken: the great, pink birds, freckled in their reflections and farther away animals coming to drink, nimble gazelles. And they stood there in silence before the beauty of the world. On the other side of the river an elephant raised its head, spread its ears, raised its trunk and they stood there in silence before the beauty of the world.

The women sat down; their backs were broken, their legs worn out. They decided that this was plenty; they would from now on be content with the paradise of water. They would raise their children in it; they would engender the race of fishermen, a delicate, long-limbed people in slender boats, a race of fishermen whose movements were swift and nimble. They wanted to wash clothes here; they wanted to carry heavy jars on their heads; they wanted to fill basins; they wanted to watch the water flow; they wanted to irrigate the sand. They wanted to lie down on the banks and stick their heads in the water. They wanted to die here, die, their faces in a hollow of transparency, die, drowned in beauty.

Who speaks of dying when there is eternal life? exulted Brother Emmanuel. But the women balked; they did not feel cut out for eternal life; dying was plenty for them; dying was their absolute and they couldn't see any farther or any higher. The men exhorted them to keep going. They had only reached the first circle, and though a few of the littlest ones wanted to stay and play with the shiny fish, the older children felt strong enough to go anywhere in the world.

Before taking off again Brother Emmanuel ordered a purification. He went into the river and they all followed him; there beneath the rising sun they immersed themselves three times. The birds flew away and on the other bank of the river the gazelles retreated in a quick surge like a wave. When the people came out they saw that the water was brown and muddy where they had gone in and that the sand on the beach where they had waited was devastated. They could see that they were not yet ready and the women agreed to keep going. The sun rose higher in the sky and they walked on; all wet, their robes stuck to their skin and outlined the women's breasts; drops of water shone in their hair and on they went, light-footed and radiant with silvery light, and Brother Emmanuel was triumphant.

They crossed a great desert that was nothing but sand, sky, and silence. The wind rushed through the dunes and drew signs on them. So the men stopped. They remained standing, as trans-fixed as trees struck by lightning, like sentinels of eternity. They wanted this gold and azure to be the blazon of their virility; they wanted the wind for their words and the signs on the sand to be their writing. They said: We shall die here, our faces turned to the sun. We shall die here because the desert is like eternity; it has no beginning and no end and we are here in the eternal place. The desert is like fire; it consumes and purifies; this is where we stay. But the women and children exhorted them; they were only at the second circle. If so much beauty existed why renounce seeing the next . . . They went off again and were ashamed of the marks their too-heavy tread left in the perfect sand, and the wind that had now come up swirled golden dust around them.

They told Emmanuel that they had gone through the second circle and not received any purification at all. Emmanuel did not reply. The troop muttered in the wind; they wanted to know where they were, not on their material and geographic path but on their spiritual path. Because after water, it's fire . . . Then drops began to fall; they were soaked in a few seconds and the sand drank up the water coming from the sky, which was running down their bodies, and when they turned around the desert be-hind them had vanished; the sand had burst into infinite, endless flowers.

They went into the forest; they walked between trees that made them dizzy. They shivered when they looked at them as if they were on the edge of a precipice; way up in the sky they saw the tree's hair as torrential foam. Because the top of the trees was moving like the sea. They were walking on the bottom of the ocean, in silence and calm while, thousands of feet overhead, storms were raging. They were moving forward into a deep valley all full of shade while frenzied clouds raced through the sky. They were creeping toward the center of the earth, beneath volcanoes and rivers, under the sea itself... And the light, bursting between the fantastic trunks, lit them with its long, hard rays, and it was like an aureole.

They were exhausted and had no more to say. From now on they would no longer stop as they willed; they knew that their powers did not belong to them, nor did their courage nor their will nor even their lives. They realized that confronted with God's design they had proven only that their minds were stupid, ignorant, obtuse. They had thought they understood; they had thought they could interpret signs that were beyond them. Whereas God was demanding only that they follow Emmanuel, not even consent to do so but follow through some inborn impulse set in motion right at the beginning. They were not to move forward but to let themselves be moved forward, let God's strength and will pass through their arms and legs, through their lumpy heads, like a woman carrying a child who has nothing to do but just let the child grow; and--women know this even better than men - letting is already too much, you have to be the growing child.

In the area around the savanna they were greeted by lookout monkeys crowning short, round, thorny trees. Seeing them in the distance, the monkeys shaded their eyes with their hands and the trees shook with spasms of excitement. We were like the lookout monkeys, they said to themselves, nervous about the future, always expecting fear, always perturbed . . . And the monkeys saw the long troop go by, all walking in time, wordless and not throwing rocks at them, so the monkeys had only their own fear and excitement to deal with; they went back to their stations, already on the alert to catch sight of some troop of men who might appear on the horizon and never go by again. They were going to wait from generation to generation completely absorbed in pointlessness, their watch henceforth absurd.

The savanna was laid out in a gentle, round, grassy landscape, composed of small things, tufts of fragrant herbs, thickets in bloom, great solitary trees sprinkled like seeds in the wind. It was in the savanna that the animals lived; in the distance you could see great herds of them racing by, followed by flocks of birds, and it was breathtaking as the wind, as the space, as life. The children asked to have cabins built with all the wood they were finding. And the men and women would have given in to the children's wishes, because the savanna is a pleasant place to live. There was less grandeur here but an air of peace and freedom and hope that made it human. But Emmanuel didn't want to because the final circle was still somewhere else. Where? they asked. Emmanuel dug around in his memory.

The final circle was exactly beneath a great red tree, in the middle of a village, near the ancestors who were smoking in the hut where they held their discussions, with cackling hens and the yellow bitch with the pointed muzzle, lying on her side to rest her pink, milk-swollen teats. He was taking the troop to the village. And the troop, seeing the trees shrivel, the grass collapse, the water dry up in the puddles, the animals change their nature – the troop, hearing the spitefulness of dogs and the fatuousness of roosters, saw rage sweep across Emmanuel's face.

He looked around in search of Queen Mab's tall silhouette and didn't find it. When questioned, the others said that she hadn't come, that she had never left the banana plantation. Some of them said more specifically that she hadn't gone any farther than the village well. Emmanuel's face became distorted. Woman, the bringer-forth of madmen, she had abandoned him. And he cursed her. Behind him the troop of the blessed just stood around; he felt their sadness and their fatigue. Emmanuel continued on with the march.

Suddenly his foot ran into a rock and he recognized it; in his heart a great massacre took place. Because it was neither the time nor the place. He was on the road but he hadn't gotten there yet, and the stone he had run into was like all the rocks in the world, just like the one next to it. But this was the stone with which he had struck and this was where he had killed. He thought about the clear beauty of the first circle and his conviction, he saw again the brilliant perfection of the second and his joy, he remembered the majestic order of the third and his hope. Here despair had not changed by a single cry, not batted away a single tear.

Here, he told them. He wept with his same adolescent tears, with drool, with mucus, with huge throaty sobs. Here. And they went down on their knees. Suddenly they could go no farther. Suddenly they could no longer see, no longer hear, no longer understand. Here, said Emmanuel. They took out the white powder. They were in a hurry to be done with it. Emmanuel showed them what they had to do; he emptied the can into his hands and brought his lips to it the way you drink from a spring, and his mouth filled with powder, he cried: Woman, woman, you have aborted me . . . and I no longer have a name.

Ballad of the Monkey

The sidewalks of the lower city were jam-packed with people . . . They passed penniless Tutus, cigarette venders, dealers in stolen whisky, as well as peddlers of statues hastily antiqued with dirt and wax: an entire, squatting population all waiting for the Japanese revelers or drunken sailors to come out. Hearing the music grow louder when a door opened, in a single bound they leapt to offer their services then folded back up and dropped to the ground again as soon as the guy disappeared around the corner with a sulky Tutu woman at his heels. Victor sat down in their midst facing the Coco Bar; in front of him he placed his iron and his toaster. Too expensive, said the sailors, these being the only words they could say. Hello, *too expensive*. Got a cigarette? *Too expensive*. A hundred francs a trick, *too expensive*. But then they paid twice the price. Too expensive, they said to Victor, but they took his toaster and iron because they usually took whatever was there on the sidewalk: cigarettes, statues, girls, and even children. *Too expensive.*

Hugging Alexis close, dark against his dark suit, Victor followed them into the Coco Bar. There was no big window or little ones, either, just a door to push open; inside it was very dark. He asked for a beer; they handed him a can and he remembered the first evening at Guastavin's. He drank with great glottal spasms, you could hear the beer run down his throat with a big, deep, regular sound that hurt. Alexis woke up and looked up at the can; he thought it was milk and reached his hand out to have a bit.

All of a sudden, as if an electrical current ran through them all, the Coco Bar discovered the monkey; and the sailors squeezed together to see. They were already laughing just thinking of the funny spectacle monkeys supposedly provide. They bought him a beer. Alexis drew back uneasily from the can; he hid his face in Victor's neck, where he became more confident and peeked out from under with a sidelong glance, extremely tempted, which made the spectators laugh hilariously. Finally he detached himself from Victor, stuck his lips way out, which meant he was curious and greedy but felt intimidated and yet wanted to be polite. Bursts of laughter and shouts as well. Then he opened his mouth, uncovering his teeth, and gave the little hoarse cry that meant he was afraid. And all the men surrounding him made faces back at him.

Victor drank Alexis's beer; he gave him a drop on the tip of his finger. Alexis licked it and clicked his tongue; the crowd couldn't have been more delighted. Three sailors suggested to Victor that they would buy him "to give their buddies a good laugh." They imagined the faces in the dormitory when a monkey was discovered in the quartermaster's bunk: *rape!* He's a baby, said Victor, but nobody cared that the monkey was a child. Just being a monkey equipped with four arms and genitals, even a tiny one like that, made him a sexual animal, adult and ready to fornicate. He's still very little, Victor insisted.

The sailors were from the crew of *The Dreadnought*; it was written on their caps. Maybe they could get him a space on it? It made Victor very happy to think that the imaginary tall frigate topped with white canvas that had delighted his childhood had a mirror image in an armored submarine with too short a nose and that the winged sailors running up the halyards had been transformed into lead soldiers. He asked when they would be getting under way. Tomorrow, said the sailors, wrapping their arms once more around their Tutus with a touch of regret. An officer waved him over. He was extremely interested in Victor's problem, all alone in this big city. He straightened a lock of the young man's hair on his forehead, almost a caress. If it were only up to him he would certainly take Victor along, without the monkey, he specified. Why? asked Victor. Because. Did you ever hear of anyone in the veterinary services? But they wanted to take him. You bet! They would have abandoned him. Much obliged. The MP burst into the Coco Bar and ordered the sailors out. Tomorrow, the officer reminded Victor, whatever you do, don't get your hair cut.

The night was serene; Victor and Alexis walked away from the port and back up the river. They stopped to rest in the coconut grove edging the city; the coconut trees in silvery bracelets gleamed in the darkness and headlights from the cars swept along the river banks; the big city was all aflow with light, crackling with sound. If Alexis had been older he would have left him here, between the shadow and the light, between the jungle and the city, in a place that was no longer wild but that was not yet civilized . . . but the monkey couldn't survive on his own. Then Victor dropped to the ground. Leaning back against a coconut tree he took Alexis to his bosom, closed his arms around him; with his head on the little body, they were as one now.

At sunrise Victor opened his eyes; he was like a wounded man regaining consciousness on the battlefield. All the night's promises had vanished. Instead of coconut trees with the reassuring and nourishing shade he had expected, he discovered long, headless shafts and, between the trunks, voluminous rags, damp and black, swinging in the morning breeze. Saprophytic vines were growing on the trees, emptying them of their sap; lianas stretched out until they were covering the coconut grove with a vast net that trapped the birds but also all the sky's sediment, gas from the cars, smoke from the factories. The bracelets around the bases of the coconut trees were evidence of recent, already bygone days when rats had been the only threat. We're not going to stay here, said Victor, but it took several hours of trying to find a passage before they could get out from under the net.

Every day, at the fringe of the coconut grove, an incredible number of dead or dying animals were to be found – brought by the night, then left behind as it withdrew. With its first rays the sun dried them up. All that remained on the ground were scorched shapes, small and dark, with skeletons like fish bones. Yet they never stopped climbing up toward the open air, toward daylight, even though they had no strength left, as if their slow, stubborn migration through the coconut grove had exhausted them. They must have had a distant memory of the light and the land before the spongy lianas established their dark order.

When they reached the road afternoon had already begun. It was farther to the zoo than he'd expected and Alexis was clearly tired. Victor picked him up in his arms again. The monkey clung less tightly than when he was a little baby; he was more confident. I like how you feel, Victor told him; he liked this little round shape nestled in the crook of his arm, he liked this weight, even the slight pain caused by contracting his muscles to hold on to it.

I'm leaving you and you are my love. I'm leaving your white belly where I love to lay my cheek, I'm leaving the bluish bend in your arm, I'm leaving the heel of your foot, I'm leaving every one of your fingers and there are a lot. I'm leaving your perfect round head that fits in the palm of my hand, your ears so thin and so cool between my fingers, I'm leaving your little face. And he told him: Beautiful eyes, beautiful forehead, pointed chin, silvery mouth, and he was leaving all this sweetness, all the tenderness as well. He was leaving with the hand caressing back and forth, he was leaving with the cheek that he rubbed against the little bulging belly, he was leaving with his mouth and his nose, his face buried in the monkey's hair, breathing, licking, his eyes full of tears, and you could hear the monkey's careless laughter, his laugh for play and happiness, and Alexis took Victor's head and hugged it against himself with so much force that he ended up on top of it.

Monkey on his head, eyes covered by monkey arms, Victor walked. He was blind and the monkey on top was his guide. Then Victor unfastened the arms and put them under his chin. He walked along, wearing a hairy black hat, and the monkey's hands hugging his face were the chin strap. There are real trees here and you'll be happy in them, there's air, there's sky; and he gave names to the universe for the monkey while Brother Emmanuel's song resonated inside him. Alexis, who was now straddling his shoulders, had put his head against Victor's head; we're Siamese twins, thought Victor, then he put his face right next to the monkey's and their eyes lined up so they both saw at the same level. We have four eyes, Victor told him and, as if he understood, Alexis put his hand into Victor's. Yes, Victor said, but we have many more hands than a double creature like us should reasonably have.

First they visited the zoo to get an idea of what it was like. Except for the fate of one muddy hippopotamus and two scrawny wolves, order and cleanliness seemed to prevail. Victor asked to see the director, who at first wouldn't meet with him, played hard to get, then finally came. But that's a monkey, he said. Yes indeed, said Victor, proud as could be. But what do you expect me to do with it? At first glance it had seemed to Victor that there weren't any monkeys there. You're kidding, said the director, there are even too many. Nobody is interested in them so we put them in pens out back. I'm going back to France . . ., said Victor.

And you want to get rid of it! You're all just the same! The director went off on a long diatribe about people who adopt animals and then abandon them. It had reached catastrophic proportions. Nobody counted the parrots forgotten in the park anymore, nor the monkeys abandoned in the coconut grove, the crocodiles slipped down drains, the snakes dumped down rubbish chutes. It delighted the tourists to see a parrot perched on a street sign in the middle of the city or a female monkey crossing an intersection with her baby in her arms. The guides warned them about the snakes threading their way up and down elevators. They took it as a happy sign – How lucky you are! – that nature was so strong that it had not yielded before concrete and steel . . . Fat chance. Three-quarters of the zoo animals, if you exclude the Siberian wolves, have come from the city itself. They're abandoned animals hunted down between the buildings by city people. They brought him lame gazelles caught on car fenders, rare birds stunned when they ran into windows reflecting the sky, obese crocodiles stuck in pipes, warthogs smothered by plastic bags . . . And then the monkeys!

Monkeys were the ones who came through best when abandoned. They naturally followed people and, just like them, invaded the city dump. Surrounded by seagulls, in the constant flapping of white wings crackling like uncontrollable fire, they competed with the people on the dreadful pile of daily garbage that they call the Mountain here because it towers above the city. With their four legs they moved faster, with their four hands they picked more things up, with their powerful jaws and sharp teeth they opened and tore things apart, with their thick, sharp nails they scratched deeper; they could go everywhere with their tough skin and rough coats, numb to the fact that iron hurt and rust was poison. They were already up on top, at work helping themselves first to the best parts while the ragged women and children wasted their last strength just climbing the pile of garbage. The men insulted them and the monkeys, who were at the very top, glorying in their strength, threw rocks at the people and bits of bone and their laughter squawked and cried with the seagulls.

They had become so sure of themselves that they took it into their heads to make use of their teeth and fists to drive the humans from their shacks. Some of them had gone to the supermarket, discovering that it was easier to take the merchandise before it had rotted and been carried by garbage trucks up two hundred feet above sea level. Others wanted to have a taste of good times at the beach. One Sunday the people watched a rude and noisy, shaggy cohort descend on the mouth of the river, onto the greenish, stinking banks where the children were having fun diving, swimming, or fishing. That set off something of a panic. The men had complained and denounced the monkeys to the police, who one morning they had come with nets, cages, trucks, and guns.

Many died. Rumor had it that there were as many as five hundred corpses, which was excessive. The survivors were here, behind barbed wire . . .

He isn't wild, said Victor, he knows some tricks. Show me, the guy asked, interested all of a sudden. He knows how to eat with a knife and a fork; he knows how to drink from a glass; he knows how to say good morning, good evening. Boring, said the director; they all know how to do that. If you had told me he knows how to read and write, he knows how to talk. You can't ask the impossible, Victor apologized. The monkey in his arms looked an awful lot like a monkey; unconscious of the effect he was producing, he scratched himself a bit, casually, so he wouldn't waste time not feeling some quiver of sensation, even one caused by a nail on his skin. This is how he is, said Victor, running out of arguments.

Fine, leave your phenomenon here. The director pressed his hand down on the monkey's neck; he knew how to handle him to avoid the teeth and nails. The rough, wild feeling this caused pleased Alexis and he burst out laughing. They led him to the monkey pen; there were dozens of them, every age, every weight, which persuaded Victor that he was right. What would he have done with an Alexis who weighed over a hundred pounds, with a flat mug and a receding forehead behind heavy jaws, his childhood destroyed?

But Alexis had never seen monkeys, his mirror image was that of humans; he saw himself in the radiant faces of the children who came to peer at him, in the pale face of the red-lipped woman, and especially in the beloved, adored, cherished face of Victor. Loving Victor, the monkey thought he was Victor, or at least thought he was like Victor. These beasts, because beasts they were, terrified him: the hair, the teeth, the eyes, everything about them was monstrous, frightening. They didn't have clothes, their eyes didn't blink, their mouths didn't speak. They were awful!

Panic stricken, Alexis peed. The urine ran down his legs; he peed and peed. And only afterward did he howl because the director had dropped him. Alexis cried like a baby; standing upright on his legs with his arms stretched out, he cried as hard as his lips would cry. Victor rushed over to pick him up again. Leave him, said the director, an adult will adopt him, and Victor saw a big male monkey, disturbed by the shrieks, get up and run full tilt to throw himself on Alexis and carry him off. He's going to kill him, Victor cried in horror. No, on the contrary; that's a good sign. You wanted him to be happy. And Victor, who could still hear Alexis crying, wondered if your first experience of happiness came screaming like that.

Happy End

The news broke at breakfast. Ysée had asked that it be served to her especially early because she expected a busy day. It was there in the headlines of the *Journal*: "The Dead from the Devil." Instant shrieks. Preparations for action. All the girls were called to an emergency meeting in Madame's bedroom; they came staggering in wearing the curlers they had slept in, their masks and tooth straighteners – not pretty. They didn't understand; they rubbed their eyes and stretched; it was too early; their emotions weren't awake yet, just their very gassy bodies, their yawns, and their need to pee. That's the way these Princesses woke up: first pee, then open your eyes.

The paper was spread out on the bed. Ysée was beside herself. But what came over them? It was such a peaceful banana plantation! Poor César, poor César, doing that to him . . . She saw them there in the photos taken from a helicopter; they were strewn about on the ground and already swollen. Were there really that many? Eight hundred, said Ysée, César has lost eight hundred guys, just like that, all at once. What did they do it with? Belle-Beauty asked. With White Spirit. The girl, terribly pale, stroked her cheek. Madame was wondering if they shouldn't put off the party, when they would choose the one to be the current Miss. I'm going out of my mind, said Ysée, if somebody doesn't tell me what to do, I'll go mad! The election of Miss Sunset completely down the drain! If you put it off, tell me.

The first message didn't come until early afternoon. The girls weren't hungry. Getting up so early had taken away their appetite. And they didn't want to go take their naps without knowing whether or not the Miss choosing was going to take place – understandable, you must admit. Gilbert finally phoned. "No problem," the affair would take place; the men had found the solution. But how is César? Ysée inquired. The other didn't answer. The phone had cut off. Girls, everything's fine, she said, and then the girls, who were very tense and getting a little bored with the crisis, all gave a whew! of relief. So, to bed, ordered Ysée. But the news had made them wake up; there was no stopping them – they had to know all about it. The phone again, César in person. It's César, it's César, Ysée called out to the girls, now all ears, as if this might concern a survivor. Well? Well? Ysée asked. Well, this is shit, he said. That I can well believe, she granted, agreeing. Do you want us to put it off? she asked him, but in her heart she was begging: No, no. She knew the man she was talking to; her question had just spurred him to new courage, or at least it gave him the chance to express it: Come on, Ysée, have you ever seen me throw in the sponge? No, she whispered. So what do you think? Don't know, she said in a pleading voice. Well, I'm going to come. Organize a raffle. Hooray, girls! she cried. The rest didn't much matter. He told her that they would dig just one grave. Just one, for eight hundred? Well, what about it? As if she had protested. But hearing the raffle was announced, she wasn't going to question anything, even that eight hundred people could be comfortable in a single grave. Jushaf to make it wide, said a girl who was doing her best to follow the conversation. Of course, why had she not thought of it, a single, very wide grave, very deep and covered with dirt. Justhaf to set the bulldotherth to it, the girl went on. Justhaf to . . . But what's the matter with you – talking that way? The girl took out her retainers.

Belle-Beauty let the hairdresser in. The color of her hair needed no adjusting whatsoever. Finally we've got it! and she smiled at him in the mirror. It was hard to get platinum – somewhere between gold and silver. He put a sort of cap made of pearls on her head; it streamed down her forehead and her cheeks, down onto her neck, and made her shiver. She was ravishing. But it hid her blond hair, which was so perfect. He hesitated, took off the cap and tried some light sprigs instead, a sort of flower bouquet . . . It was less sophisticated but also more ordinary. You look like a bride. Decided. They went back to the cap and chose a simple band of silver lamé to finish it off. The manicurist did her hands and her feet. Belle-Beauty flopped down and leaned back on the cushions of her armchair. Her satin peignoir slid down her thighs and she couldn't hang onto it because her hands were a mess, all covered with creams and colors. It exposed a breast and then a thigh, all the way up to her hip; underneath she was naked.

The woman who did their makeup brought in the box of contact lenses that the girls called the Eye Box: almost turquoise blues that gave them eyes like a doll's, green ones that gave them the glare of a panther, and gold ones, the weirdest; Belle-Beauty would never wear those, as if once when she had worn them she had had the experience of seeing what monkeys see – a dazzling world of absolute sun. She didn't like the sun as much anymore, or at least she didn't like for the sun to consume her eyes. She

167

chose blue lenses; she thought they went with her hairdo. You're right, the beautician agreed, as always. And Belle-Beauty smiled. She stretched out a little more comfortably on the chair and spread her arms and legs to dry her nail polish. The peignoir slipped aside, exposing everything. The beautician looked right at her body and said: you're good-looking, Madame Belle-Beauty. It was an observation, unemotional, the opinion of a specialist.

The maid had put a white lace, merry widow corset out on the bed along with beaded stockings and the long court cloak trimmed in white swansdown. You're the most beautiful one, Madame Belle-Beauty, besides there's nothing like white; it's a sure thing – you'll be the one to win. She had to do things for the others. Coiffed and painted, Belle-Beauty stood and walked over to the mirror; she opened the peignoir and studied herself severely. No, it was *not* perfect; she still had that: a brown fleece: curly, bushy, and thick. It made a shadow under light dresses and showed through thin fabrics. So she took her fingernail scissors and snipped away, and when her pubis was no more than a triangle of stiff hairs, she shaved herself meticulously with a razor. Her genital lips created a mark on the whiteness of her belly, as if the bleached skin had split there into these pink and gray folds. She ascertained, with the coolness of a clinician, that it could all be fixed, and taking a bit of Scotch tape, she closed the lips of her sex like the edges of a wound and stuck them together.

To Port-Banane, he said to the driver of the yellow taxi who pulled up in front of him.

To the Sunset? the driver asked.

No, to Port-Banane, Victor replied.

You're not going to the Sunset? Everybody's going to the Sunset tonight, all the men. There's a big bash there, said the driver, putting the car in gear.

No, I'm going to African Resource, Victor replied.

Not the same, guffawed the driver.

No, it's not the same, and the driver felt there was some sadness in his voice.

So, first you go to the Resource and then after you go to the brothel. That way you do the whole deal.

Victor paid him. The driver gave him his change and said something else that Victor refused to understand. As he crossed the threshold of the Resource he retched. Beretti was in France recruiting directors and Papa was nowhere to be seen. The mulatto man pointed to the glass box in the back. It was covered with a black sheet; Papa now required darkness. They had made cutout stars in the cloth. Are you coming? the mulatto asked. No, I'm leaving, Victor replied. I've come from the Model Village. Model Village, where's that? The mulatto man, trying to dredge up what he could remember, couldn't see where. Victor was about to launch into a long explanation when the mulatto woman hauled herself out from behind the cash register and asked him: Are you going to the Sunset? Then added bitterly: All the men are at the Sunset tonight.

At the Sunset the party was going full tilt. Lots of smiling Banana-men, all worked up. You could see Gilbert's red shorts there in the midst of the tuxedos. Victor saw César with all the people rallying around him, giving him a good time, as well as some other fellows who had come to the plantation. A girl was going around among them selling raffle tickets. For the "Devil," she called out, in aid of the "dead"! What prizes are there? one of the Banana-men asked as he put his hand in his pocket. A super jackpot, she whispered, the girl of your choice, all night long, for your whole life. The men were buying whole books of tickets; they showed them to César. If this doesn't get you back on your feet! All this! César smiled, looking tired and tense like people who have been expecting some great calamity, some great joy, and it's finally happening. I told you so!

If the girl hadn't stood there right in front of him and insisted, Victor wouldn't have bought a ticket. Which one? she asked. He hesitated, he looked for something ending in o. She didn't have any. Cheapskate. Skinflint – he could see that in her eyes. Don't you want a 7? she suggested. Why? he asked. He was getting suspicious, suspicious of the girl, suspicious of 7. Because everybody knows, she replied, 7 is lucky. He took the number but wasn't satisfied. He waited for her to give him his change. Gilbert, to teach him a lesson, bought the rest of the book, the whole thing, all fifty tickets minus the 7. They heard a trumpet sound, blown by black heralds dressed in short, gold tunics; the curtain went up on the governor's great, formal staircase, which provided the only scenery. *Election of Miss Sunset!* The whole bar applauded, fidgeting with excitement. The girls rose in tiers up the entire flight of stairs, one on each step, gorgeous. There were pink ones, their hair arranged so they looked like bosomed sphinxes; blue ones wearing turbans of tulle; green ones covered in beads; yellow ones crowned in gold; mauve ones blooming with violets . . . There was one white one with short, platinum hair bound with a silver headband; her long, immaculate gown was trimmed in gossamer swansdown; the split in her skirt with its flowing train revealed white stockings held up by a garter of orange blossoms. Why, it's the Dame de Montsoreau! exclaimed a little, atrociously old man as he took the proprietress by the arm. Ysée calmed him down: Yes, yes, it's the Dame de Montsoreau. It's the Dame de Montsoreau, he repeated weakly and fainted dead away.

Down below the guys were shouting and it was almost more than Madame Ysée could do to hold them back, begging them to look before consuming, the way you try to postpone cutting into a particularly successful wedding cake. Then and there, at that moment, you could tell she was proud of her girls, top and bottom ones alike: clean, demanding girls, girls that America would not have disowned, girls beautiful as few actresses ever are and decent as they never are. It wouldn't have taken much for her to produce a heartfelt tear from her one eye; the girls were her masterpiece, the glory of her life, the redeemers of all women.

The crowd was growing impatient. Gentlemen, gentlemen, there's plenty for everybody... The tickets had been collected in a champagne bucket in the shape of a top hat, a black iron contraption, heavy and lethal. They asked who was going to draw the winning ticket. Ysée, Ysée, chanted the crowd, and being a good sort she sacrificed herself. Taking on the airs of a magician, she waved her hands like wings to show there was nothing in them, then she stirred the bits of paper around, pretended to take one, put it down, and took another that she held out to the crowd. You can be sure they adored her in that moment. What a woman! César murmured. The crowd fell silent, in awe. Ysée unfolded the paper, read it to herself, then, looking all around the room, she announced the number. The Banana-men examined their stubs: a hundred, two hundred, a thousand stubs suddenly worth nothing any more.

Ysée saw a very handsome, very blond young man wearing an incredible black wool suit stepping forward. A letdown. But the crowd seemed to be taking it well; if that's the way it is, it might as well be funny, and the stranger was funny. Victor felt himself picked up and carried through the audience by a surge of manly brotherhood all chanting: The boy, the boy . . . I'm a man, he thought. The white woman, he said, pointing at her. The white woman, the crowd chanted, the white woman...

As he climbed the staircase toward her, he smelled the sweet scent of the pink ones, the coppery fragrance of the yellow ones, the mild concoctions of the green ones, and the violet fragrance of the mauve. When he stopped in front of her the perfumes died away; she smelled only of herself, so restful. He closed his eyes. When he opened them again he saw so much happiness in the girl's gaze that he recognized her. Lola! he moaned. Victor, she sighed. He embraced her. The crowd shouted: Not so fast, not so fast. That was fine with him. He clasped her in his arms and it was the happiest day of their lives.

In the European Women Writers series

The Human Family
By Lou Andreas-Salomé
Translated and with an introduction by Raleigh Whitinger

Artemisia
By Anna Banti
Translated by Shirley D'Ardia Caracciolo

Bitter Healing
German Women Writers, 1700–1830
An Anthology
Edited by Jeannine Blackwell and Susanne Zantop

The Edge of Europe
By Angela Bianchini
Translated by Angela M. Jeannet and David Castronuovo

The Maravillas Distric
By Rosa Chacel
Translated by d. a. démers

Memoirs of Leticia Valle
By Rosa Chacel
Translated by Carol Maier

There Are No Letters Like Yours
The Correspondence of Isabelle de Charrière and Constant
d'Hermenches
By Isabelle de Charrière
Translated and with an introduction and annotations by
Janet Whatley and Malcolm Whatley

The Book of Promethea
By Hélène Cixous
Translated by Betsy Wing

The Terrible but Unfinished Story of Norodom Sihanouk, King of Cambodia
By Hélène Cixous
Translated by Juliet Flower MacCannell, Judith Pike,
and Lollie Groth

The Governor's Daughter
By Paule Constant
Translated by Betsy Wing

Trading Secrets
By Paule Constant
Translated by Betsy Wing
With an introduction by Margot Miller

White Spirit
By Paule Constant
Translated by Betsy Wing

Maria Zef
By Paola Drigo
Translated by Blossom Steinberg Kirschenbaum

Woman to Woman
By Marguerite Duras and Xavière Gauthier
Translated by Katharine A. Jensen

Hitchhiking
Twelve German Tales
By Gabriele Eckart
Translated by Wayne Kvam

The South and Bene
By Adelaida García Morales
Translated and with a preface by Thomas G. Deveny

The Tongue Snatchers
By Claudine Herrmann
Translated by Nancy Kline

The Queen's Mirror
Fairy Tales by German Women, 1780–1900
Edited and translated by Shawn C. Jarvis and
Jeannine Blackwell

The Panther Woman
Five Tales from the Cassette Recorder
By Sarah Kirsch
Translated by Marion Faber

Concert
By Else Lasker-Schḷer
Translated by Jean M. Snook

Slander
By Linda Lê
Translated by Esther Allen

Hot Chocolate at Hanselmann's
By Rosetta Loy
Translated and with an introduction by Gregory Conti

Daughters of Eve
Women's Writing from the German Democratic Republic
Edited by Nancy Lukens and Dorothy Rosenberg
Translated by Nancy Lukens

Animal Triste
By Monika Maron
Translated by Brigitte Goldstein

Celebration in the Northwest
By Ana Marĭa Matute
Translated by Phoebe Ann Porter

On Our Own Behalf
Women's Tales from Catalonia
Edited by Kathleen McNerney

Rosie Carpe
By Marie Ndiaye
Translated by Tamsin Black

Music from a Blue Well
By Torborg Nedreaas
Translated by Bibbi Lee

Nothing Grows by Moonlight
By Torborg Nedreaas
Translated by Bibbi Lee

The Museum of Useless Efforts
By Cristina Peri Rossi
Translated by Tobias Hecht

Bordeaux
By Soledad Puértolas
Translated by Francisca González-Arias

Candy Story
By Marie Redonnet
Translated by Alexandra Quinn

Forever Valley
By Marie Redonnet
Translated by Jordan Stump

Hôtel Splendid
By Marie Redonnet
Translated by Jordan Stump

Nevermore
By Marie Redonnet
Translated by Jordan Stump

Rose Mellie Rose
By Marie Redonnet
Translated by Jordan Stump

The Man in the Pulpit
Questions for a Father
By Ruth Rehmann
Translated by Christoph Lohmann and Pamela Lohmann

Abelard's Love
By Luise Rinser
Translated by Jean M. Snook

Why Is There Salt in the Sea?
By Brigitte Schwaiger
Translated by Sieglinde Lug

The Same Sea As Every Summer
By Esther Tusquets
Translated and with an afterword by Margaret E. W. Jones

Never to Return
By Esther Tusquets
Translated and with an afterword by Barbara F. Ichiishi

The Life of High Countess Gritta von Ratsinourhouse
By Bettine von Arnim and Gisela von Arnim Grimm
Translated and with an introduction by Lisa Ohm